THE MELODY OF MY LOVE

Set me as a seal upon thine heart, as a seal upon thine arm: for love is strong as death . . .

Song of Solomon 8:6

The Melody of My Love
© Migena Ramaj 2014

First published in Albanian under the title:
"Melodia e Dashurisë Sime, një Poezi Gjaku" © Vernon Publishing, 2011.
Tirana, Albania
ISBN: 978-9928-104-09-0

Translator: Erjon Ramaj

Editors: Marie Notcheva
Randa Montgomery
Brunilda Rustani

Introduction by Dr. Teuta Toska

Printed in the United States by CreateSpace, Amazon Publishing ®

This book is dedicated to the people in my country, who are suffering from this drama

Contents

Introduction

"**The Melody of my Love**" is the third book by Migena Ramaj, a long prose, while her literary activity has mainly been in the field of poetry. She is editor-in-chief of "Ilira", a seasonal magazine for Christian girls and women, and she has also worked as a journalist in Radio 7 for several years. The author was born in Bajram Curri in 1978, one of the most important cities of northern Albania, situated in the Tropoja region. The story she tells serves as a small window of insight into what has happened for centuries in the lives of the people in this region, people who have governed themselves in their remote and impenetrable villages in the northern mountains, away from the authority of any invader or government.

This book, starting as a romance and ending as a drama, shakes the reader with the truthfulness and everyday-life feeling of its pain. The events happen in a city in northern Albania, in the country's most tragic year, after the great political changes of the '90s: 1997. The people of the city where Melody, the main character, lives are again being governed by their unwritten law- the Kanun. Revenges forgotten by time, forbidden by the dictatorial regime, condemned only in appearance during that time, are again "coming to power". The year 1997 would add to the tragedy of this exhumed phenomenon, as a result of the political anarchy the country was going through.

That year, due to an extraordinary economic slump and a financial fraud of national dimensions, many people lost their savings and "attacked" the state. Abandoning themselves to anger, the people attacked almost everything public, in order to steal, destroy and disintegrate. The climax of this madness was when crowds of people attacked the military warehouses, ravishing the military's stored "riches", from work tools to weapons. Almost every Albanian family was equipped with a gun: some to sow terror and violence, others to defend themselves from the first group. In this collective madness, human beings had only one goal: survival.

Abruptly, within a night, with the opening of military warehouses, all conflicts were exhumed from their graves. Now everyone could solve his conflict, even the most random one, with guns. In the north of Albania, the situation would be twice as hard, due to the Kanun of the mountains. The centenarian lack of a state has made it possible for Kanun laws to find deep roots in the soul of this society. Family, marriage, parenthood, inheritance, properties, work, honor, guests, and even messengers are defined and arranged among mountain people by the antique law. But its weight is felt especially in the manner in which the Kanun "arranges" for the issue of murder. "The blood is never lost" (Kanun, 917)[1], and its avenge will ask for the life of "males from the murder's house", even if that means a newborn boy (Kanun, 900). A murder, according to the law of revenge, is not a simple crime: ironically, it is a relief for many men isolated within their houses for fear of being targets of revenge, and at the same time, it means the isolation of dozens of other people, waiting in "hope" for someone to become the next holocaust (sacrifice), bringing

about their liberation. The isolation of dozens of men means the ruin of dozens of families, and, for innumerable others, it means spiritual destruction, anxiety, misery, and depression.

Besides the main theme of the book, that of blood feud and what this phenomenon causes to the soul of Albanian society, the reader probes the deep battle of every human soul that appears in the book as a character between life and death, love and hate, good and evil. This battle is played openly in the daily realities of the characters of "The Melody of my Love". And, like in every simple life story, the first to face this life-threatening phenomenon is love.

The book turns into a daily drama happening in the lives of ordinary people in this region. It is a voice raised to unfold the absurd tragedy in which men and women of Northern Albania and beyond are thrown every day. This social phenomenon is not mainly an issue of ethnographic studies, a subject of governmental social policies, or the "attraction" of funds for dozens of non-governmental organisations - it is the wound of thousands of families, a phenomenon that is daily challenging the lives of so many people. Beyond this, the readers are urged to take a stand for themselves: what will they do with blood feud? Will they raise their voices? What will they do with murder? Will they forgive it? Will they seek self-justice? This small book shakes every reader to their core with questions such as these.

The protagonist of the book, Melody Gjokaj, a high-school student, falls in love with a new classmate, Ermal Korinaj (Eri). Their love is an ordinary event, common to all young people at this age, but it becomes extraordinary when faced with blood feud: the Kikaj family, a family that enjoys some power in the city due to their involvement in politics, declares blood feud to the Korinaj family (Eri's family) driven by a very old conflict. Immediately, the love between Melody and Ermal becomes a "luxury", something of second-hand importance, even an obstacle: but can love be an obstacle? Life or love? Death or love? What will Eri do? Will he sacrifice his life and his love? Or will love save his life and his heart?

The narration is conceived as a diary in some parts, and as an epistle (a correspondence text) in other parts. In this way, the reader can go beyond the events of the novel to analyze the soul of characters who suffer a dramatic transformation brought about by death and hatred. The high poetic register of the narration, as well as the chosen genre (that of a diary), give the language of the book the shape of a poem. Through the dramatic and painful events narrated in the book, the reader can comprehend the weight of blood feud in the life of a society. Thus, as the author has united life and death, love and hatred in these events, the book turns into a blood poem.

Dr. Teuta Toska

The Kanun of Lekë Dukagjini, Shtjefën Gjeçovi O.F.M., "Kuvendi Publishinh", August 2001.

An Unexpected Love

Hello Eri,

It has been four years since you left, but the words spoken on the way out sound as strong now as they did then. I reflect on your cuddles even though they hurt, and now for the first time, I respect your silence. These years rise unacceptable before me. How rapidly they passed! During this time, in the midst of people, I have been alone. The strengths of what I felt about you grew in letters, and were renewed in memories. Today, after four years, I stepped for the first time into our school. It is odd how a spiritless building holds so much value and the empty halls so many words and dreams–so much life! Do you remember how much noise we made while waiting for our classes to start?

It was almost a month after school had started when you were transferred into our class; one of those classes that made the headmaster proud.

You didn't look nervous at all the first day, in that familiar hoopla of our class. On the contrary, your eyes gazed on us as if *we* were the newcomers. With the passing of the days you quite naturally became comfortable in our midst, faster than we all could have thought.

Only you know how you managed to get everyone to like you, just like a property, or, how may I say it, a garment; like a robe that you put on so naturally, or like something that belonged to you–that's it!

I feel I see you even now seated in the last desk, raising your hand—with your sleeves rolled up–to answer. In the beautiful darkness of your face and pitch black hair, lay your crystal green eyes. The guys looked forward to staying in your company, while the girls doused their curiosity by listening to Lira talk about you. Within record time, you managed to become our weak point.

I am convinced that we admired that distinct confidence in your character. It looked as though nothing could threaten you, and no one could even come close to you.

Meanwhile, here entered the other character - me.

Lord, thinking back to that time, I feel as though I am watching the sequences of a movie that is not without thrills; scenes that I am playing and replaying. I see them; I relive them in these years.

At that time, I was lovingly given to the life of books. Unbowed before dreams, I published prose, poems, articles for the newspapers, magazines, even though half of them would echo nowhere. I liked to think it was because of the dysfunctional mail delivery system. Better to console myself in this way, right?

My professor, Engjëll[1], inspired me with the idea that one day the world would honor my talent. In this way, he encouraged me to persist again and again. What could become a barrier for me? I was like a volcano that nothing could stop.

Writing was my hidden, untouchable cave; it was my triumph. Nobody, not even words themselves could display the almost divine feeling that moved in me when I poured myself into the letters. I was transformed before them, and together with my heart that beat strong before the trundles of the time, I decided to perform miracles. I regarded the conversations of our friends and their dreams as distant. I had surrendered the today to the tomorrow, only to obey my heart and write. I had decided who I wanted to be, and I lived like that person should live.

How good it is that life does not always consider the formulas of the mind! How much love would remain unlived if it happened like that!

This is the background in which you found me, such was the time when you started to shift my attention–almost without my noticing–from the books that were holy for me, to you. I can't remember which one of us started that play of glances, but I noticed that you would settle your eyes on me, and with the same strength you pretended as though you were not paying attention.

I couldn't even believe that this was happening.

"Mel, this is a whim you've come up with," I would repeat to myself in a whisper at school, and aloud at home. After all, I was too far below . . . you . . . but, let's suppose it was happening that way. Again this tiny feeling had to be suppressed without coming to life, had to die without being born. Ohhh, had I time for such games?

Anyway, I could not hide from myself the shiver that would be presented to me from your soft peeking, though while our glances crossed, I quickly shifted my glance somewhere else. Sometimes just to convince myself that your gaze did not give any emotions to me, any shivers, I stared at you. But that gaze went immediately to my heart, only to rest there. Even the trifles took on meaning just to connect with you, to cling to you, to make you the center of my attention.

I need only to close my eyes tonight and turn back to that bowing salutation that greeted me, as a prism of rays released in one intimate piece of heaven. Far within my flesh, in that perfect harmony of the soul, love was coming to life. It grew bright, neatly connected with your versatile temperament, with the humor that threatened the situations but never the people, with your eyes, hair, voice, words, movements, gait; with everything that I could and could not see about you; the love that spoke to me in silence made me fragile, yet it gave me strength.

Quite naturally, on an ordinary day, you came close to me with your straight steps, and the voice that conveyed confidence.

"Melody, I have read every article, everything that I could find of what you've written. Even though everyone speaks about your talent, I wanted, let's say, to be convinced myself. In fact I admire your way of writing. Everything that you create has life in it."

"Thank you for the appreciation," I replied with nervous emotion. "This is very kind of you..."

". . . buuut, but,"

"Ah, there is a *but*," I said, as if all came tumbling down with it.

"But I would gladly read more of your compositions that aren't yet published," you continued at once, "only if I would be given the chance."

"Hmm, I am afraid that after reading all that scribble, your opinion would not be the same anymore." I added, seeking for a way out.

"Yes, I assure you," you answered with one breath, "one can gain something, even from a single conversation with you."

For "poor" lovers, the normal conditions resemble magnificent ones; the most natural glances betray; the most common words come as tremendous emotions.

The pleasure and the gain were mine; yet I had an inner place where I hid my sensations and all laid there, without sounds and words, as something precious, but under a layer of unbroken ice. Only the glances would resist it.

My days suddenly turned most attractive. A person cared for this, a person that was nothing for me, but that was turning into everything. He would naturally leave all of his friends to stay where I was staying; he presented me with seemingly modest things that, in time, turned into the souvenirs of my feelings; he bought newspapers, magazines, and books that could somehow serve me or just inform me; he organized celebrations and surprise parties; all these with such fine attention that not even the most overseeing eye would dictate, but that I had to understand. He was trying to bring to light in me that which I was trying to hide.

On one of the days, as we were becoming closer, he, in the most polite way, asked me to dedicate something "to our friendship":

"Whatever comes easiest, even a note. I want to save it for the time when you, surrounded by crowds waiting for your autograph, rightly won't remember us."

You know what, Eri, your request at that time hurt my pride a little, the pride of a girl who was expecting one thing, yet was asked for something else. That's why I almost exclaimed to you that I had plenty of compositions dedicated to friendship, since I considered it an important part of life.

"I have seen how you appreciate friends," you replied again, restful and bold, "but let's say that in my selfishness, I am asking for something apart from the others."

Well, this was too much; a very bold self-estimation, I thought.

Anyway, that night, while I discussed this with myself, I clearly understood that . . . I understood that all of my being was enlightened under the gazing of your eyes.

Truly, how much you have given me with so little. I was ecstatic every day under the emotions of meeting a guy I had known for only a short time.

But, if in silence we are the real us, in life we remain actors. And as an actress, I could not share this emotion; this new roaring in my heart that filled me with you. I was afraid to allow my feeling to fly away, even though it was born quite some time ago, and was now living stealthily. I hid myself behind this play, and with it I also hid the first verses that my heart gave me, replacing them with a formal scribble. The next day, just as we finished the last class, I hastened to your desk with a piece of paper in my hand.

Naturally, you read it in one breath, since I was just walking off the school property when you called to me to wait for you. You came close with the paper jumbled in your fingers.

"I am a good friend, right, Melody?" you asked, sounding angry.

"Oh, thank you for the honor!"

"Is this all I am to you, Melody?"

Leaning on the wall with a confused attitude, I looked at an Ermal whom I didn't know, and somehow inside, I rejoiced seeing him that way. In front of me he stood—he who made all the school girls lose their minds. And furthermore, he who made me lose my mind.

"Friendship," you whispered after a while, "is but a crumb, compared to what I feel for you, Melody Gjokaj. I've seen in your eyes, this mutual feeling of mine," you added, focusing on my eyes, as you would find support there, "but unfortunately, I have been lying to myself," you said, dropping your gaze again.

I loved the joy that your face, writhing with humble gestures, brought to me. You were humble before me, therefore I did not peep. I just dreaded that the life of this happiness would be short.

Why should you pursue a feeling that would not be returned to you? I didn't know of a girl in our school who didn't feel caressed when you greeted her. I didn't know of a girl who was not trying to be noticed by you in any way possible.

However, since that day, you became the afternoon gallivant under my balcony. Your persistence not to leave until you could see me and greet me, caressed my heart. Could I resist?! Why did I need to?!

Look at what was written in my diary at the time . . .

"Today we also stayed together. The thought that he will be the last whisper of my lips, is my peace. I play like a child; I act like a happy kid whenever I am with him. His name, "mountain

wind", pours into my heart, demolishing everything else. Without knowing, he inspires in me a desire to be different . . . to become a better person."

What happiness I lived in those days! How crazily happy I was!

Neither happiness nor sadness, neither love nor hatred, failure nor triumph, are equally worthy, and even their intensity is almost not the same, if they are experienced alone. The uncontrollable desire to share it with loved ones is something between the thought to exhilarate someone else, and the need to share this new thing that makes you even talk to yourself. I talked to everything that did not talk, because "at the least," I wanted to tell the whole world about you. No matter how it was, of course, to Lira, your cousin and my childhood friend, my best friend, this would be joyful news.

Only with the light turned off one night in her room, did I manage to tell her how the most precious feeling of my life had started to blossom.

"I've met a boy, one whose smile calms me," I succeeded to pull out, after a series of forewords and hints of a secret.

Oh, I can see Elira even now jumping on the bed like a child who just received a gift she was not expecting. Sleep came to us only in the first hours of the morning. Finally then our voices, enticing dreams of the future, started to reduce.

Today, sitting again at my desk, I was without Lira, without you. In the midst of my soul's orientations, the desire to write to you crouched in my mind.

This is the only thing that I still manage to do for you.

Eri, seeing what has been going on within me, I don't know how much you will recognize me, just as I don't know how you have changed. Even so, I will try to share with the Ermal in whom I found myself. I say so, because walking these years without you, the waiting has anguished me. The anxiety had every right to enchain me because no signal threatened it, even to shake the silence just once.

Regardless of this, I waited. I waited on the intimate presence of a piece of paper with one line on it. I waited to hear the sound of your voice whispering my name somewhere behind me. How many times I instinctively turned my head, looking for you!

How could I know that between our different worlds, the coals of loving did not diminish? Does love for the person of the heart diminish as the sun goes down, leaving only the rays, then the shade, and in the end, just the memory?! You are growing in the place where the rays of the sun warm the night of my place. I stand there, almost where you left me, in the same lanes, the old apartment blocks, the same streets; I am being built by the same people.

The idea to write to you won me over, because I so want for you to learn, that through these years I have been searching to lean on you. Where are you? Are you far away? ARE YOU VERY FAR AWAY?!

While we were acquiring shape, as the clear yogurt that is formed in the mold, we were split cruelly, without strengthening the shape of what held us together.

With lightless eyes, you confessed to me that you were leaving Albania. You had my hands in yours, while pleading contritely:

"I will come back . . . I promise . . . I will come back for you. We will be together. We will be together just as we have dreamed, right, Mel?" You continued following me with a steadfast look. "Will you wait for me? Will I find you here again, as my own?"

Eri! You had taught me to be loyal to my heart. I did not know how cloudy or sunny life would look upon us. But I knew that in myself, I would try in every possible way, to be with you–to be FOR YOU.

So far, until this day, I have remained in the light of the words:

"Yes, in every way, and with any price, I will wait," I said, knowing well the power from which I was drawing these words.

With your silhouette running away , you kidnapped my closest friend. You erased the very breath of life which urged me to inhale air and to continue walking every day.

For what reason should I walk now?!

Shadows from the Past

I came back to our hometown for my teaching practice; however, I feel more like a pupil. I awoke late, with hardly enough time to get ready. In the meantime, Mendi, with his sleek hairstyle like a fascist, was calling:

"Mel, aren't you ready yet? Since you have the honor of being accompanied by me, at least hurry up."

"Which sweater suits me better? The sapphire one? Or should I try the black one?" I teased him.

"Dear sis, I don't understand all this concern for your appearance. Who is going to put his eyes on you when I am beside you? Ohhh, they will stop when they see this rising star, who happens to be your brother. Bah, soon I will have to hire bodyguards because of my many admirers."

I stand in the house as a person who, after a long and tiring road, desires to sleep and not wake up, to wake up and not remember, remember and not get hurt.

Maybe it's for this reason I find myself on this typewriter.

Alright, Eri; now we are going back to the dawn of the day that would change the course of my life. I confess that is one of my most familiar memories. It is like an illness; people tend to turn back to exactly the same place where things started to go downhill; they turn as lost in the desire to erase that episode; they turn, desperately, blaming that small piece of history for what it brought and for what it ripped from their hands and control.

I was taking it easy, and got up slowly from the bed.

"Mel, sweetheart, wake up; a new day is waiting." Meanwhile, a shy bell interrupted the series of caresses. The hand became braver each time, and the bell fiercer. I heard Mum's footsteps near the door.

"Ohh, who could it be at this early hour?"

Mum came in my room, fuming:

"It is Ermal, the son of Luan Korinaj. Why did he come before the dawn?" She kept speaking, while I was confused, and didn't know what to wear.

"I have no idea, Mum. I'm sure he only has an errand from Lira," I answered with all possible calmness.

"Let Lira be more careful," she continued. "What if the neighbors see you? Imagine what they will think. Or will they even hesitate to speak?! Mel, at this early in the morning, I have no pleasure in giving what you call moral sermons. But I don't want gossiping behind my back, especially when it's about you.

My body was trembling all over, and I tried to be as calm as I could, so there would not remain a trifle of doubt in Mum, because after this, she would figure out all on her own.

As soon as I left her eyes, I ran breathlessly into the outside hall.

"What is this visit at this hour—" I started to say, but the shadow on your face made the words fall backwards. Your eyes were wet with tears, and from the uncomfortable expression of your face, I understood that you had been forsaken by sleep.

"Eri, what happened?" I asked, fearing what I could hear. The long moment during which you sadly rested was so heavy on me. Then you came toward me, saying:

"Mel, I am sorry that I came this way, so inopportune, but I had to see you. I won't be in school today, and I am not coming tomorrow either, maybe never again. I preferred to tell you myself . . ."

"To tell me . . . what do you want to tell me?" I added in the anxiety of a person who has perceived the undesired and greatly hopes to be mistaken.

"My family, I mean Daddy, Rubin, and I are being pursued for . . . an . . . old blood feud," you blurted out in the end.

"What?" I said in a whisper. I thought that my voice would instantly die.

"Until yesterday, I didn't know . . . that . . . we were involved in this kind of history," you continued with a frightened tenderness. "To save our lives, we must isolate ourselves. And perhaps you know that, wherever we are, we will live in fear, because according to the Kanun[2], they somehow have the right to kill us.

Lira had already trusted me with this anguished secret that threatened the life of her only uncle—of her only relative she accepted and recognized from her mother's side, the life of the only man in the universe for whom she, without a questioning blink of her eyes, was ready to do everything. She had confessed it to me, when you were still studying in Tirana, near Rubin; when I did not know you and I couldn't foresee that one day this would separate me from the love of my heart, that it would lead me to attempt suicide; that this would incite in me the most real despair which a human being tries to live through.

In that place, in front of the hall, at that moment, I heard the rasp of the leaves quivering on the century-old oaks, the whiff of the breath of mountains before us. I saw the long, beautiful necks of the cliffs that I held so close to my heart, and I was terrified by the reality that in this vast universe, we human beings dig to find or create ways to hurt one another.

Among the mountain wind, even today, as that morning, as tens and hundreds of years ago, there still travels the calamity of a former time. The time of blood feud! It has neither time nor place here, but we ourselves raise it from the dead. We hold it on its feet; we give it back its youth, even though it is rotten.

As a highlander, I knew very well the meaning of these words. I knew the tragic puff stinking from the words: "We are in a blood feud." But I was part of one of the few families who had not inherited such a debt. This fear did not walk into my life, so I could easily be considered as "favored by fortune".

My girlfriends had quit school and worked the most vulgar jobs in order to maintain their families. They had said goodbye to their dreams for life, only so they could provide food for their brothers trapped in the house. My fellow citizens wiped away the blood spilled on the sidewalks because of blood feud, and I frequently heard people justify the murder of my peers under the mask of, "He avenged. May he be honored!"

But never, never had blood feud come so close to me as that day; never had it touched me.

I felt the need for words to give you strength, but what could I say?! A thousand ramifications of fear penetrated my brain when I visualized our life from now on.

I couldn't stop the tears. I bowed my head to hide while the tears flowed down my nose and all over.

Eri, you were the first human being on the planet for whom I would hold all my breath to serve. But here it quietly unfolds–the barrier to separate you from me; a chain that rarely did anyone disconnect and "remain alive".

Days later, I pondered all those things I could have said to somehow calm your despair that morning. Silently the sounds paced. No words could form to show the closeness of my heart, as that leaning, as that resting of my face on your shoulders, as that hug that caressed all my cells.

"Unexpectedly and senselessly, your whole world narrows, and is wrapped inside the problem you are facing. And wherever you wander, you think only that, recognize only that, and live only that.

Even the tiniest of troubles can find its way into our lives, and like a snowball, little by little it rolls over and becomes an avalanche. Slowly this avalanche slides forward within us; and suddenly it becomes so startling, so large.

Now I enter Lira's room, like I do every weekend.

Furnished with such finesse by her uncle, for me it remains simply a dreamy room. From there we invent rich opportunities of entertaining. I invent, she confirms! The sun grows old on us as we wrap our heads and feet with blankets and sit on the veranda.

"Why this gloomy face?" I whisper near her ear, because tonight she is a little lost. She breaks off watching the city, and looks as though she can find the answer in me—whether or not she should speak, and she waits, waits, until finally she starts:

"Mel, I will trust you with a secret. My mum's family has an old enmity. The problem is that even if you track the world palm for palm you wouldn't meet wilder beasts than those with whom they are in enmity. I am speaking about Flavio's kindred."

These words stab my heart, because Flavio is my best friend, and this isn't unknown to Lira. Each time that I have striven to demolish this gap in between the two of them, I have failed.

"What do you mean? What kind of enmity are you speaking of?" I ask her, with a heavy look that wants to disagree but also dreads.

"We are in a blood feud with them," she starts again, "from a lifetime ago. It has returned as history, not long ago, when Mum accidentally heard the chatter of her employees. She heard that the Kikaj family has re-sworn to avenge. But now those aren't just whispers, at least not to Mum. It has turned into an obsession for her; everywhere she goes, it seems as though people whisper only about this. But my uncle appears to be totally unaffected."

"We have the best properties, assets, and scholarships for children. I would be troubled more if they didn't talk. It is simply a human jealousy, even a very justified jealousy," he says, trying to calm Mum. "You will be convinced yourself that it isn't anything more."

Lira stops for a little, as if slowly releasing the sadness that compels a weeper. But she cannot stand to look like one who weeps so easily, so she goes on . . .

"The tragic beauty in this is that everybody has forgotten the origin of the quarrel which has brought tragedies generation after generation. What was the cause? Anyway, since about fifty

years ago, or maybe even more than that, when my grandfather avenged his father, we have been in debt. Now it is my uncle's turn to pay . . . with his life."

Yes, you can call this, a curse.

"My grandfather killed, and as the custom and the moral code of the time demanded, he took responsibility for the murder. He was then handed over to the authorities. With good behavior, amnesty, and because in those days a vengeance murder wasn't considered a crime of high degree, he had hoped to see his wife and children again. But it didn't happen that way. After a few days in prison, someone told him the bitterest truth that ears on this earth could ever hear—truth that managed to absorb and devour his life—his only brother had escaped from Albania. He had passed the borders into Yugoslavia, trying to secure his family's life. In doing so, he sealed the destruction of those left here inside the borders.

"People say, Mel, that overnight, every strand of his hair turned gray.

"The tomorrows of his wife and his two children would be lived, there where the ill-fated were deported with the mark 'Persecuted'.

"Day after day, these thoughts obsessed his brain until he had a nervous breakdown. With that extinguished light in his eyes, word for word, with the same tone, with the same shadow in his face, Uncle often recalls:

"If it wasn't for Mother, we never would have come out alive from those camps and those terrible villages. If I managed to live, it is only because of the strength that she gave me, even with just a look. I don't know where she found the strength to make her lips smile, but she knew how to revive my hope with that smile of hers. She would hide her food ration, and save it until she found the chance to give it to me. Every day she caressed me, if not with her hands, at least with her smile."

Lira continues, "You know, Mel, my uncle still keeps a pair of trousers that my grandmother patched with strands of her hair. Can you even imagine living such a reality?! And to think that my grandmother grew up with servants at home! What traumas have fallen on these people! Her last words were her desire that my mum and uncle would never separate from each other. That's why they preserved that amazing affinity."

Ok Eri, I will "pause" here, because I feel I should clarify something. I was accustomed to a jovial Lira—a person who couldn't stand in just one place; able to inject enthusiasm everywhere and to everyone. Truly, I was the friend of her confidences, the friend of her most intimate and explosive moments, and despite this, the Lira I saw that night I had never met before. This case I had to call unique. Lira was downhearted, as if irritated in her weakest point; the point where every one of us is transformed into a biting snake, even if we were usually lambs.

There isn't a human being that doesn't fear something, right?! Just like the enthusiast, also the melancholic; just like the human who hides somewhere behind the stage, or a man worshipped by crowds: we all fear something—a feeling, a person, a tomorrow, or a past, when we lie down to sleep or awaken from sleep.

Today, I know I can say it is a fear that started in the beginning. There, in the Garden of Eden, a "nudity" that the poor human patches as he can, but just patches it.

I was the other edge of Lira's temperament, but I preferred to "degenerate" into someone like her. She talked with people she couldn't even stand, but made them think she cared deeply about them. And when an idea crossed her mind, she headed toward it fast as a storm, even if this meant going against the entire world.

While her voice trembles, she strives not to allow her tears to go down her cheeks. It wouldn't be a sin for her to burst into tears! I don't believe there is any cure that melts the heart like the tear does; it shows you are human.

But it does not happen. Her gaze angers, and at the same time she raises her voice:

"That's why I behave that way with Flavio, and you criticize me for being heartless with the feelings of that peasant. The strongest love that I might have towards him is hatred. Even babies who carry that last name, the children in whose veins flows Kikaj's blood, I hate them with all my being."

Now yes, the Lira that I knew had been awakened.

"Ah, if they disappeared, if the earth would devour them, I would be granted the greatest pleasure I could ever enjoy. They don't deserve to walk or even step on the same ground as we do."

Her eyes turn, softly staring, while she starts to speak of what she is passionate about, her family.

"Then in my uncle's life came a ray of sun that shone gently, as after a storm. He married a girl from the same class; from the "privileged" class of the persecuted, and so did my mum. In the old tower, my uncle slept and awoke with the dream to fill every corner of it with the sounds children. As an inside howl that dream has followed him, as last wills follow us. Life gave him Rubin, Eri, Diti, and his 'little niece', as he calls me. He even said to me once that I was a soul-daughter for him. Oh, my uncle reads even my thoughts! Even without opening my lips, he knows what I am going to say."

Sleep makes her still with dewy eyes. She talked and talked as if she had lived there among the camps disgraceful for their purpose; as she was there, when the tower near the city, that witness of the slain from the bullet of blood feud, was restored and transformed into a fairytale villa; there where the children grew up, one after another; there where Lira's mother mourned in the graveyards her insane father and her heartbroken mother . . .

Today, quite different from that night, I find myself part of this drama. Today my chest fills with the spasm and the fleeting thought that one day Eri, my love, could lose his life because of this ghost called "Kanun". Today the despair is whole inside of me.

Even the hidden whispers of sleep bring him closer to me. In every angle of my heart, he stirs. Even though I study for my graduation exams, I am swallowed by all the letters Lira brings to me every week. My whole day meanders in them . . .

Learning to Hate

"Mel, my Melody, have I ever told you how much I like this name?!

You are the most beautiful gift that life could have given me.

For two months I have looked at the sun from the small windows of my house, and even so, I looked only through quickly stolen glances! I miss seeing your face. I miss your eyes, Mel, and it puts my heart down not knowing when I will be able to freely see you again. I fear losing you like I fear losing my life. I don't think that your family will allow you to build a future with a man involved in blood feud.

And how can I blame them? You deserve much more.

I pass the time reading; I even try to walk with the pace of classroom lessons. What else can I do? I listen to our favorite songs and go deeply into them. I allow myself to get lost and taste (and why not?) the need to have you close even for one moment. Even just seeing you would be enough!

This is a little out of my day.

Diti, my younger brother, comes to me as a rainbow between two dark clouds. He is everybody's rainbow. Few are the moments that revive us. They occur when Diti and Dad come around the house and make a mess when they cook, being guided by recipes and cookbooks, and when we are robed as spoiled girls, they serve the food to us. These are the small moments that bring to us what we have long forgotten—smiling. Dad becomes Diti's teacher and parent; he plays as Diti's peer and talks with him as a friend. Dad lives for Diti.

Again and again, time remains empty. The hours just hobble on.

Everything seems overshadowed, unjust, without a tomorrow. Cursed be this "Kanun" that punishes us for someone else's faults! Why should we be what we're not, and do what we don't want to do? For whose sake must this sacrifice or this estrangement be made? In the name of which religion, of which virtue?!

Our house has lost all the warmth that a home normally has. It resembles more a weapon warehouse. Pistols, rifles, machine guns, hand grenades—only tanks are lacking. During these days, even I am learning to use a gun.

First you remove the safety, then open the bolt handle, and fill the chamber with bullets. After you close the latch, you take the shooting position, remove the safety, and with a little "luck" in that finger on the trigger, you can even take the life of a human being. I detest touching guns. I detest this situation in which I find myself captive. Nonetheless, in the nights of never-ending darkness and waiting, I feel how hatred rises in me and I can't cease it. It starts, especially when I fear for the life of my dad and Rubin, when I think of Diti's isolated life. Then I see myself not hesitating to revenge, or to be "a man", as highlanders say, because some of them like to justify murder.

Mel, your letters are the air that I lack. At least I can salvage this time with the feeling that would not be dimmed even if I was free or bound, if I stayed inside or if I strolled every corner of the "outside" world.

Adoring you,

Ermal"

The hatred is becoming as pus under the skin of Eri's life.

I breathe for him and even try to live his sensations each time a leaf in the wind starts to make noise, or any blood-thirsty shadow moves in front of his gate. Behind those rails await armed people, who breathe his air with the desire to devour it forever. Lord, I feel the heavy beatings of the night hours, as though they might be his last—forever. I wait for that terrible gun, about which I am ashamed even to write. I am embarrassed when I catch the strings of my thoughts, but I hope it kills somebody else and not the one I love.

I write to him every night. Every night I pour out my heart in my duty to save him from falling, to save him from hatred, to ease his longing for the sun rays, for the crystal air of mornings, for the noisy conversations of friends. I want to be the melody that calms his spirit.

A Friend's Goodbye

The circumstances in which I happened to be then and until this night that I write, taught me to love even the smallest and most ordinary moments of my time alive, to laugh about things that once I neglected even smiling about . . . because, if I leave today's laughter for tomorrow, tomorrow might never dawn.

Blood feud would not restrain my passion for you; neither friends, nor enemies could touch it.

Lira took on the job to put this whole situation under control, and whenever this happened, I stayed calm. Aside from delivering our letters, she brought to me the image, the desires, the longing for you; she escorted so accurately the reflection of your face. When my heart weakened and the rumors stormed around me, I ran to her for a dose of encouragement.

Courage is especially charming when love unleashes it, but her courage was unleashed by hatred, a fervent rancor that discharged especially on Flavio's face.

Do you remember how Flavio fled from your presence? Where you were, he had no place. Where you went, he left. When you spoke, Flavio silenced. I knew it wasn't an ordinary teenager's jealousy, even though you were the last to arrive, and took everything. Deep down, I knew that Flavio could not behave differently, however I could not understand his indifference towards the boy that drew everybody's admiration.

That saddened me, because my feelings for that person were putting roots in my heart, and at the same time I saw a dear friend whose value paled so much that there came to a point when I couldn't remember what had connected me so much with him, or what I had found so valuable in that person. He remained as an outfit once beloved, now forgotten in the darkness of the wardrobe.

I felt him constantly further, but also feebler, more broken. There were times when I asked him what was going on, but even in those times I accused him of shutting me out of his life.

Before you came, not a corner in Flavio's heart that was foreign to me.

When you were locked in, he almost quit school. He came increasingly less frequently. Those few times that he appeared, Lira made his day a living hell. She waited for him at the classroom door as she, "her majesty", had tended for the "welcoming ceremony". What didn't she invent?! She fabricated the sort of things that only a few girls are able to create. The whole class busted into laughter, and sometimes they only laughed at Lira's imposing presence.

Flavio did not react. He never used the power that every guy would use to shut the mouth of an impolite girl. I was so sorry about Lira's attacks on him, and it really irritated me. Lira's insolence made me angry, and so did Flavio's gawkiness, because Flavio was as much accused and as guilty as you are, Eri.

Especially pricking my heart were the moments when Flavio had to "welcome" the gibes of the teaching staff, because heavy is the word of the uneducated educator. A teacher's word can raise you or make you fall. There is no limit to what a teacher can build in a child's life.

On one of the days that my eye caught him in the school environment, while I was going home, I saw Flavio coming towards me. We hadn't met for quite some time, not to mention spending time together.

"Can we talk a little bit, Mel? I want you to know this is the only reason I came to school today," he said, a little shy.

I walked close to him to let him understand that I agreed. Seated on the benches in front of the school, in the shadow of the hundred-year oaks, I started to hear the noise of a tempestuous river of life, the river that was swallowing my friend's life. He talked to me as if I had never disregarded him, forgotten him, or put him aside.

"My cousins rightly push me to help them revenge. Grandfather wasn't theirs only. You know, Mel, my uncle's sons have baptized me with the name of "Wretch". If you hear the neighborhood boys calling out this name, don't be surprised. They are calling me. The only shelter where I put my head is my family. They do not condition me. Maybe this is the privilege of being an only child. However, now more strongly than ever, I feel the absence of a brother or a sister. My parents are treated like rags to clean the ground on which the "moral" people step."

He cracked his fingers, strolled his hand through his hair, and restarted,

"For my extended family I am as good as dead, I am judged as insolent and insensitive to the kin's shame, I'm even a stain in itself."

And then he fixed his gaze on me, continuing,

"At school, in the midst of my childhood friends, I am judged on why I am this person, or more precisely, why I chose to be born exactly into this family, why I pre-chose this kinship, why my cousins dredge up this old blood feud—it does not matter that this happens around us ordinarily—why we harm the man Luan Korinaj, to whom everybody bows. Maybe they suggest killing somebody else? These people are so defiled! On the one hand, they don't even allow you to walk in the same street with them without making you a killer; and on the other hand, they don't allow you to walk because you *have* become a killer."

Time after time he clenched his teeth, wrinkled his lips with an innocent and cloudy look, as of the man who doesn't know where to sink. He stopped for a bit and then continued,

"How can I blame my family when people are blackening their lives? The feet of the dishonest step on our honor, the mouths of the harsh offend us."

But is Ermal's family to blame?!

While I listened to him and while I went far back in memories, pure fear rose up in my heart.

There were some underground strings—they were the mind, the arm and the dynamics of a mechanism that could not be seen, but that dished and spanned a terrible scenario eagerly awaiting to be put into motion. A mysterious foreboding started in me. It hurt me, whispering that "everything, everything was bigger, more terrible, much more frightening than we could see".

"Mel, it will sound absurd, but in everything that I am going through, what are especially hard to swallow, are Elira's insults."

After he rested for a while, he added,

"The most beautiful irony is that I can't hate her, despite what she does to me."

"Don't tell me that you still have feelings for her?" I jumped. "Forgive my reaction, but . . ."

He smiled lightly, "Don't worry, I am surprised too, but this has not helped me take her off my mind. Naturally, you remain the only person to know."

In the end, Flavio's gawkiness was explained. That's why he didn't react. Dozens of times I had thought of going close and shaking him hard by his shoulders, reproaching him about why he stayed silent and allowed being humiliated when he had no fault.

"Mel, I want you to understand something. My cousins truly believe that if they avenge, as is happening frequently in these times, they will walk proudly in the midst of people, especially now that we are entering manhood. People judge this is the perfect age for revenge. We are living in times when people have as their own law, even as their conscience, the opinion of others. More than from uncles, they are urged from society. It teases them, it depreciates them. Friends offer them information and even money. The people exclaim every day, 'Hey, isn't there something new? We can't wait to 'congratulate' you and shake your hand! You still haven't done anything, right? Oh, don't lose patience! That's how these things work, they need time. Alright, good luck!' Society takes your soul while you're still alive, and there is only one way to get rid of them: killing. The whole kinship is fighting to put in its place this underhanded honor; this dignity that needs bloodshed to be gained," said Flavio, strengthening his voice as if he pulled himself together, "and one way or another, believe me, they will succeed. Few people know what my cousins are capable of doing."

If they succeed to revenge by killing themselves, then yes, this would make the fulfillment of their dream, but if they don't succeed, a lot of money is ready to be paid for the head of one young Korinaj. And when this happens, I prefer not to be around. I can't stand Elira's eyes when they fall upon me as upon a disgusting thing. She makes me feel guilty for being born into this world; this world where she walks. Then . . . why hide it, I feel sorry for Eri, too. He isn't my friend, but I never really considered him an enemy. Anyhow, this desire is not enough to change the course of life.

"But it's not your fault, and not your responsibility," I protested, "If it depended on you, nothing evil would happen to them."

"Why are you so sure, Mel? Have you ever experienced being pointed at in the street? Being mocked by friends and enemies, relatives and strangers? Have you ever gone to buy something, and were treated like a handicapped person? I pray you never fall into the crowd's hands!"

"I wanted to say that people know your family is different from the rest of your kinship; everybody knows that you don't mingle with filth of this nature," I added, now with a weaker voice.

"First of all, these things are not filth for 99% of the society in which we live our daily lives. Then, Mel, if they know I don't mingle with such filth, why do they despise me?! It is useless . . . anyway… besides to talk, I am here to bid you farewell. I will leave here, Melody. I have found some people with whom I will be leaving for Greece. Or at least I will try. I'm leaving tomorrow."

I felt like yelling like never before, just like the spirit that forces the voice to cry because something very dear to it is being crumbled.

I was nestled in the spectator seat from where I watched a dear person who tottered in one of life's most entangled, most tragic, and most forgotten labyrinths. He tripped, fell, and desperately sought the way out, while I… ah, yes, I took out my handkerchief and dried some tears. What else could I do?!

Looking for something that would make him change his mind, I turned the subject to Elira. I searched and wanted more than anything another chance to be close to him, to be his childhood friend again.

"Let's talk about Lira. Why don't you tell her yourself what you feel for her? He who loves, be it in the most hopeless manner in the world, must at least once show his feelings," I reasoned, raising my voice.

After he stood up fast on his feet, as if at the end of his patience, he sat once more almost on his knees. He gently took my hands and continued with the words that still tonight keep my heart fearful for him:

"I am thankful to you for this conversation, Melody. You have no idea how much I missed this time. You will always remain my little sis. But there is no place for me here. Believe me, there will be less of a place for me here tomorrow."

He left as he came: slowly, shyly, alone, leaving me there under thunderbolts of self-reproach. It seemed that I could hardly find the strength to carry my bag, to get up from the bench, and to find my way home.

Listening to my heart while I write tonight, I see that people of the same heart are connected through an entangled wire of time that succeeded in making their lives a mess. It slammed them there, where they themselves couldn't do what they considered right. "The crowd", "the people", "the others", had entered the stage. They foresaw a huge spectacle that mustn't fail for any reason; that's why they themselves had taken control.

Eri, still as this letter takes the form of a journal (I could even call it a night-diary) I don't even know how it ends. I know that it grasps me, and inhales me after itself. Walking in it, I relive every event. I dive into them.

I live even where I have never been, when the Kikaj pardon the blood, when you come back, when . . . the fantasy of my desires lives in me, in every crumb of my life. Often, this fantasy has granted me one more day, and donated to me another tomorrow.

Eri, this letter is for YOU. It is taken from my heart and created to arrive at your heart, but in some way, each of us, here inside, has his/her part. This holds the name of sweet friend for me; it makes me shudder while it brings it again to my mind; it pains me while I close my eyes; it is as dear today as always, the name of Flavio.

If I should be grateful to anyone in my life, without hesitation, my eyes bring me to Flavio. During the most innocent time of my life, I lived close to him.

With Flavio I took my first steps and together we put our first words into a sentence. With him I learned to use a spoon, fork, and knife. I learned to read, to walk, to dance; I learned to grow. Ever since kindergarten, he was like a guardian angel for a tiny creature like me who spend most of the time at kid's hospital, sometimes with bronchitis, sometimes with pneumonia. He held my hand when ice made the streets slippery. When balls of snow were being thrown, he became my shield, going in front of me. He used to take me for walks when the leaves painted sidewalks yellow. He swore and got sworn at, beat and got beaten, when somebody hurt me. He helped me with the complicated math exercises that I couldn't stand. I can't think of a moment of my childhood in which he wasn't there.

"Write, marvel the world," he constantly encouraged me.

It comes quite naturally to be "special" around people who treat you so! He was like a strong-boned and terribly beautiful hand that Life had used to caress me from early on. Flavio withdrew from our affinity formed since kindergarten, to leave a wide horizon to my passion for you, even though I never found the courage to tell him about you.

In between us, secrets did not exist. It came so naturally to share with each other our sympathies and dislikes. It was a deal made by a part of the spirit itself, an agreement without ceremonies, without words, yet renewed and loved. Of course, he knew me well enough to understand my growing emotions, the feelings I was experiencing for the first time.

And, in the hardest period of his life, I wasn't there. Eri, around you, I would forget. Around you, I would not see.

And now it was late! Too late! The charring day was quietly withdrawing with a triumphant sunset.

I went to Lira. My eyes wore tears as I emptied the details of what time with Flavio had evoked. My best friend, she, whom I ordinarily tried to resemble, did not move the tiniest muscle. Heart-tenderness for Flavio she considered a disease which would never touch her. She started to laugh with an abhorrent irony:

"Again with these stupidities? Didn't I tell you that his head is empty?"

I could not understand if I hated or pitied her. Who in the world did she think she was? Who knows what kind of look I gave her, because she turned to me:

"Mel what are those "Mother Theresa" eyes? Even if Flavio were the last male on earth, I would prefer to die without knowing love, than to know *his* love."

I don't know if she had a heart at all! If yes, it was being consumed for the stately Luan Korinaj. That name alone sweetened her face, made her eyes smile, and softened the armor of her heart.

I feared Elira. I feared the enthusiasm she hated with. Within seconds, hatred transformed her completely into another person. After that, with her childhood impulse, she kissed my cheek, continuing:

"Mel, I haven't forgotten to love, but I have learned to hate also. Hey, try to understand me, please. Let's exchange places for a moment. Become Lira and imagine my mother fainting at almost every gunshot she hears. Can you then pretend to have compassion for him who makes her cry? Are we kidding or what?!"

She took a deep breath and immediately slipped into the story of her grandfather.

"My grandfather spent his life in camps and prisons, moving from heavy to heavier labor, from Puka to the mountains of Mirdita, until he was locked in a psychiatric ward, for their fault. Now, after fifty years, they want to kill his only son. Filthy kin! Tell me, where should I find compassion for them? Flavio is from the same scum, too. Don't lie to yourself."

A Letter from Ermal

I greet you, my sweetheart,

Please listen to the whispered song of birds and stay in view of doves, for me, a little longer than just for yourself. Send me their fervor in the next letter. As a prisoner, I love the freedom that has imprisoned the free, because they have it, because they don't pay for it.

I am falling day after day, Mel. It hurts saying this, but in a flash, life has struck me a horrible blow. Everything has been overturned in one moment, one moment that shuts out the light, maybe forever. I don't know if the day will ever come when I will walk the streets without fear.

I have never thought about death, though today she can't wait to swallow me. I feel like the man who said, "I knew that everyone dies, but I thought that for me there would be an exception."

I am not embarrassed to confess that I am afraid. Afraid of death. Fear of what comes after that.

The idea that our life will never go back to how it was terrifies me. My mind goes back to that afternoon, when my enraged dad took the car and left the house without giving any explanation. He traveled all night to go to my brother, Rubin. The next day, he returned with him. Fatigued as he was, he shared with us in great detail . . . this life we live today. I hated my name and last name, the grandfather that I had never known, the written and unwritten laws, the place I came from. I hated this story whose genesis everybody has forgotten, this story that slams my life without mercy.

I left very angry, kicking the doors one after the other. I condemned my father for a fault he didn't commit, I judged him for a reality for which he wasn't responsible in any way; it was a lot bigger than he was.

My mother reminded me to be grateful that my father still lived. She said that the Kikajs have shown themselves to be noble and human, because they might have not told they were going to follow us. It means that, according to "the law", they could have killed my dad dozens of times without warning. In short, we are expected to be happy they told us ahead of time that they were going to kill us. Now I know why my mum insisted on accompanying us to school, and why I was supposed to go back home immediately after class; why it wasn't good, as my parents said, to organize or to frequent parties; why my mother gave me countless recommendations that seemed absurd for my age, and even more so for the life I used to live.

I swear, Melody, I always found her sitting in the front yard my dad had so deftly worked, waiting for me, "These are insecure times" – she used to say, hugging me and escaping my reproachful look.

Today, I long to simply step in that yard.

Mel, my dad transferred me here because I was more secure close to him. Rubin was going to start studying in Italy.

With the desire to defend us, Dad and Mum had reasoned not to tell us anything. I don't know why. Maybe they wanted to postpone as much as they could the news destined to destroy our life; or perhaps they had the superstition that by ignoring this situation, by not mentioning it at all, we would be saved from it. However, my transfer here has only made the situation worse. By passing every day in front of their eyes, the hatred of my enemies has been inflamed even more. And to think that I asked myself, why didn't these people return my greetings?! How many times have I thought about Flavio!

Oh Melody, it is so heartbreaking to find Mom hidden in the rooms, red-eyed and with her hand on her mouth to quiet the sobbing. That elegant lady has weakened and changed into a faded, broken woman . . . because it could happen that one day when she comes home from work, some of her dearest people may no longer be alive.

I feel weak, powerless, and worthless. I can't do anything to save the lives of the only family I have on this earth; I have neither words nor strength to console my mother. I want to risk my life for them; I want to carry their whole burden, and save them from the anxiety that has wasted their sleep. If one of us should certainly die, I say to you sincerely, I would want it to be me.

The motive that pushes me to stay and wait is you, Melody. What I dream, what I live with you helps me to be forgotten and concealed in a spiritual secret, and it raises new hope for life in me.

Dad's friends have gone for the third time to the house of those we are in blood feud with, offering opportunity for reconciliation. Now this group of cousins has come up with the idea that after their grandfather was murdered, he was also shot in the face to be disfigured. This is a shame in itself, a disgrace for the blameless and much-honored name of their kinship, so, according to the Kanun they have the right to kill more than just one person. You know, Mel, while I say these things to you, I feel like an animal, just flesh waiting to be served.

There is no way for Rubin and I to be excluded from the revenge. Dad, forgetting his pride, asked this request imploringly. He promised not only the purse of gold that once was used for the redemption of one person, but any sum of money they might decide. With this kind of people, I am afraid that not only Rubin and I are in danger, but also Diti.

They swore that the execution of their revenge is just a matter of days, and they will treat this as if it were a case of fresh blood. Lira explained that this means a tragic murder, something too horrible to be mentioned—something that challenges time itself. Moreover, by massacring us they will turn into "VIP's"!

They have drawn out the mediators, threatening them not to go in front of them again, because they are making our situation more desperate.

Stupid people! They won't be happy in their gluttony, even if they dispersed our blood to every single corner of this city. The more polite you are on this earth, the more people tend to devour you.

Daddy makes endless calls, yells in the house, and then immediately asks for forgiveness. I never thought I would live through moments like these and see my dad so humbled. To each child, their father is like God. But to me my dad has been so even now that I am grown. It was enough for me to unload my problems on him, and then everything became immediately easier.

I still can't believe that in the sparse circle of my dad's important friends, there is not one to give us back our freedom. I don't understand anything. I don't know what will happen!

Eri

Love's Fleeing

I spent most of this afternoon with Mendi. He has grown to a beautiful stature. I almost look like a dwarf alongside him, and he doesn't miss a chance to mention it.

He stands in front of the mirror in the corridor, with the door open from side to side, and his "lecture" begins:

"Interesting how life revolves, dear sister. Once you held my hand, but now I have to sit on my knees to give you a hug. Yes, yes, I have to state that life is unfairly cruel to some," he says, as he bows his head towards me.

He turns and digs through the drawers and cardboard boxes piled in the storehouse of unnecessary things. From there, he comes back with some old sweaters. He throws them in my face with a proud look, and naturally makes his next comment—"They don't fit me anymore. Here, it's a gift. They seem to be your size. Ah, how much I have grown!" Adolescence has matured his voice and "cracked" his character. Mop–headed and with unfocused eyes, today he dedicates himself to one thing, and tomorrow, to something different. Being Dad's weak spot, Mendi gets preached at for small mistakes, but his bigger faults remain unmentioned.

It is exhausting to see your own habits and weaknesses replicated in the people you love. The flaws flaunt over you, proudly putting you down; and not only you, but also the ones you love. Even though you desire to yell, you must accept keeping silent and allowing your loved ones to fall, to get hurt, and raise themselves again, if they will.

Mendi is sweet and bitter at the same time; he is fragile and exploding, secret but pure. He is completely devoted, even to observe the little steps of a child. If he doesn't look at the world this way, things rise and fall without touching him. Everything in his view becomes beautiful, and worthy of being devoted to.

But this, for our time, is toil. This time of ours is a crazy time, because we see dishonesty being honored above candor; because what doesn't serve us we throw away, and what enters our pockets, even if it is called contempt, gets kissed.

After we finished classes, we went to *Ermal's Coffee Bar*. Only the name has remained the same.

The parties at your bar are certainly the weakness of high school memories for our former class. While the other students were immersed in dancing on the improvised dance floor, you would come alongside me, raising your shoulders as if to justify yourself by saying, "I have to stay close to you. I can't find comfort anywhere else."

Not a dream, or words, or sounds; no movement, not even a particle of life, did we want to experience apart from each other, did we? We loved even the breath of each other. We wanted to own even that, for time was short, the world was small and people around us were evil. Maybe that's why we started writing to each other then, even though we met every day- especially because we met every day.

Eri, my memories are connected to you, whether I want them to or not—outside the walls of my house and within them just as well.

Here now, I will turn to the day when Mendi pulled me to go back to the house in the middle of school break. All the way back, I kept asking him what he had been up to this time. Because that's the way it went: he made the mistakes, and I eliminated the "tracks". He would force me to swear on the living and the dead, that I had broken Mum's favorite candlestick, that I had taken from Dad's savings, when he skipped classes, that I had asked for permission, and other things like these.

With his mouth closed, he took out the key from the necklace. The most fortunate place and the most perfect solution had been this, since he had made the dream come true for the key of our house to go some weeks without getting lost. He put it in the lock, and turned it slowly. With a strong silence, he pushed the door open. In the hall, right behind the door, Lira was waiting. I also saw Diti.

Bah, all of this was so weird. What had happened? Why was Lira inside my house with the door locked? Then . . . then . . . someone else appeared—the sweetness of my days. It was you.

What had happened? Were you redeemed? Was it possible? Yes, yes, it had no other logic.

At last, you were free.

Overwhelmed by the surprise, from the emotion, from the happiness, I walked slowly until I came to the coat stand, believing and disbelieving until I jumped into your arms as in the middle of a dream. It was a gentle and fragile dream. I was afraid that it would crash in a blink. I didn't want to disturb that time with questions, or with my most justified curiosity. I just wanted to live it. Because what I had dreamed every night, and what I had desired every day, was happening! Lira and Diti had slipped away and left us alone.

"I can finally see you again, freely," you said, after you pushed me away from yourself a bit, piercing me with your look. I do not know what euphoria of feelings filled you in those moments, but mine I cannot describe.

"Oh, I feel like I am looking at you for the first time. I missed you, Mel. Only my heart knows how much I missed you."

But what importance did it have now? I had no intention of dredging up the past, and much less to mourn it. I would treat it with its name, "The Past".

Now you were close to me. What was I missing? Would I ever desire something more?!

We sat down on the floor, and just like a kid, I entered in between your arms and legs, as you liked me to. I felt your arms and body conquering and covering me like . . . like they wanted to take upon themselves something that was threatening me. . .

"Mel, I have put you in circumstances through which I never wanted you to live. I confess that sometimes I have thought it would have been better had I never known you, than by knowing you, to cause all of this pain. "

"Whereas I would always choose to know you," I said, turning my head toward you and caressing your face, "always. But why this melancholy?"

"Can you tell me how you got redeemed?"

Lira always assured me that her adored, absolute, incomparable uncle would make it happen.

I still can't swallow the idea that she kept it hidden from me. What a surprise it was to me! This will remain the most stunning surprise of my life!

I was hardly breathing from our quick talking. I was in the peak of joy, there where it seems you are going to be born for a second time; where a shining world gives you a friendly wink to assure you that this is entirely for you, and it is just the beginning.

"Melody, don't go that far . . . don't hurry," you gently spoke, after an embarrassing smile. "Things are not as you think. I find it hard to tell you though . . . no, we are not free. Everything is the same, if not worse."

I got so angry! I was angry with myself, because I jumped to conclusions so fast. I flew high with on fantasy wings, only to then collapse on the ground.

"Then what does your coming mean? How is it possible that you came out in the middle of the day? What madness have you done?"

Even now I see your eyes . . . and I can hear the rhythms of your discouraged voice:

"I needed to see you. I needed to touch you. I needed to tell you myself that . . . that . . . I am leaving Albania."

"Whaaaaat? Eri, this is . . . tell me this is a joke. Please," I said, while desperately searching for approval.

Looking pale, you followed my quivering lips, and turned to me tender-heartedly:

"I wish, believe me, more than anything, I wish I was joking, but unfortunately I can't say that. My mother's relatives have prepared everything. They bought the passport; they got the visa—in the illegal way, of course.

"In two days, I will fly to Florida as an American citizen. First I will go to Tirana to be transformed into another person, to look like the boy on the passport. Dad is in debt up to his neck. A mountain of money has bought my life's salvation, at least temporarily. After Rubin and I leave, they will put everything up for sale—the bar, the hotels, the supermarket, everything except the walls of the house."

God how fast you were speaking! Or was it me following you slowly?!

I know, that day I wasn't waiting for the phrase that closes fairy tales with a happy ending, "and they lived happily ever after", but what I was hearing was cruel. It even stole the air to my hope; it destroyed all possibilities of having you, of following you.

A life that injected anxiety into every cell, that's what I was living. In haste, my destiny was being dictated to me, slammed and overturned right before my eyes, and somebody else was scribbling it. At that moment I blamed your dad, but in time I would understand that your departure was the only chance for a life offered to you. Diti was the only male of the family who, because of his age, was not threatened. Until he was grown, the conflict would have come to a solution, for better or for worse. If for worse, Luan Korinaj's sons would live. Would your father be killed?!

While I meditate for a long time tonight, I realize that . . . he has triumphed. Your father managed to do what every loving parent in this world would do—be a shield for his child, anticipate pain, and save him from it. You lived, and this is all he could achieve. Naturally, he couldn't arrange for this blood feud not to persecute you again; he could do nothing to make it disappear. It will always be a haunting stain from the past. He dreamed about buying you the freedom to close your eyes at night as the rest of the world does, without worrying about tomorrow. He wanted an unthreatened tomorrow.

Don't people have a solution for the unnecessary taking of lives? On what edge can they hide, not to be followed by it, not to be touched, not to be alienated?

How do you feel, Eri?

Alienated?

What leads you today?

The desire to forgive, or the instinct to kill?

The need to cure pain, or the call to take blood?

I cried as much as I could cry. I cried, because in the deepest corner of my heart, I had the feeling that I would lose you. I can't remember having lived through deeper tumult in my spirit. Until then! I have to stress these words, because I had a lot more to see, a lot more to live ahead of me.

Lovers have a hardy courage. Separation makes them crazy heroes. Love completely grasps you, makes you live only for it, when it is free, when it becomes impossible. Then it lures you, and makes you happy by making you sad. It takes your breath away by giving you life. Then when hope dies, love itself gives birth to it.

Your house was surrounded by people with their fingers on the triggers during every hour of the night, and you went out in the midst of the day, challenging everything and everybody.

In those brief moments that I had you close to me, my mind spread across dozens of horizons, all with the same sun, you. The Kikajs could shoot you from a bar by the road (there, where they would make their "clear-headed" decisions); they could be guarding the area around your house. They haunted everywhere.

"Eri, you must go, before. . . well, it is time for you to go," I achieved to say, hardly breathing. In some moments, even your own breath becomes a burden.

With your eyes fixed on me like an obedient child, you threw the wrinkled coat over your shoulders and looked like an old, tired man. Your hands instinctively searched for the heavy metal in your pocket. The object you once hated.

Oh, how clearly I saw that our lives were separating here; but still, and still, and still, what I felt was strongly triumphant in every cell of every part of me. While Lira walked a few steps ahead and Diti behind, I felt like a convict. Was I not? Convicted to hide what I felt, convicted to shrink from what I was living, convicted to forget whom in every moment I was passionate about— I was revived and I lived remembering him.

Without hugging you, without touching your face or hands, without seeing the glittering of your tears, I was detached from you. Because naturally, there wasn't time to separate as we wanted to, as we felt. With my eyes conquered by tears, I saw you more faintly each second, stuck with Lira as one person, until you entered inside. Broken, I started to fall back from where my heart remained.

There cannot be a gloomier feeling in the world, than going away from where you want to return with all your strength, going away from where with all your being you desire to remain.

I hadn't walked far when I heard steps behind me. Somebody was following me. With the carelessness of a person who has endangered what the most valued thing, I turned immediately. It had been the steps of a child, the child who was infected with the disease of the mountains.

"Eri would feel better if I accompanied you," said Diti, holding my hand. He accompanied me until we came to my apartment.

"My brother really loves you a lot, Mel. He would return just for you," he told me, wiping my tears as if touching the whole pain I was going through. As he went back, I stopped in the hall to contemplate his walk.

His steps were as slow as a lamb's while plodding through a just sown field.

Life After Eri

In this emptiness and vastness of feelings, even my hand hardly obeys to paint the face of what I feel. The mirror, I meet only occasionally. My eyes have become especially shiny from the swelling and redness that tears have inscribed, and I feel like I am someone else. Everything I put in my mouth tastes like spoiled food.

"You have lost so much weight, girl!" whisper the ever-observant neighbors. Oh, how they get on my nerves!

As a wounded dog, I am provoked by everyone. Only in bed do I let my heart be desperate. In this time, my bed has become my closest friend. Where on the earth can I find the strength to detach from him?

I revive in the silence of the night when everyone lies asleep; I tighten in the bed while others awaken to the day. I remain, touching the bones under my skin. I bring and re-bring to mind that I accompanied Eri, maybe never to see him again?! If his family goes after him, there are few chances he will return. Have I lost him? Inside, oh how deep inside this fear sticks its teeth! Sadness twists with it, and I don't care to live anymore. Life is precious. Throwing it away, I fear; living it, oh, what an effort. Effort needs energy, and in these moments, all energy is dead in Mel Gjokaj's being. All my tomorrows are suffocated by the vision of Eri far away from Albania. He remains in my life the highest peak I have to reach; I only exist in order to be close to him.

A Motivated Student

A special chill of pleasure overcomes me this night while I detach from everything and sit down to meet you.

To meet you?!

These letters make me forget myself and invite you close to me. Indeed, when lost in my thoughts, I lift my head up in search of words, and it seems as though you are in front of me.

The last time I wrote, we stopped at your parting. My final graduation exams were in front of me, and after that, a fiery summer of studying, aiming at university. Half lying in my chair of straw, covered with emptiness, neither awake nor asleep, I quarreled every night with myself. I had to wake up! But how? I needed two softly staring eyes, two hands that wanted to rub me while I unbuttoned my pain.

Mendi was still too young to learn that life was a jungle in which his sister was a harmed being.

And Lira?! Lira's often irritating self-security made me close my mouth in restraint— showing neither approval nor any other feeling or emotion. Do you understand me? Lira and I often used to talk late into the night about everybody, and the things we discussed were told to no one else, but not even the tiniest flash crossed my mind to trust her with that whose memory made my breath hard. Certainly, she would advise me not to let myself down, but to gather my strength. But where under heaven could I gather it?

I needed time and effort, episodes and encounters with others, to understand that I looked wretched when I acted like her, when I "became" Lira. A person seems especially monstrous when he behaves not as himself, but as another person. The beauty which finds no meaning in being compared to anyone lies inside, deep inside a person. Such beauty is a pearl, a unique pearl in everyone.

If I am taken away by fantasy, Lira obeys logic. Whereas I follow after the feelings of my heart, reason is her God always. I can't help but move my bed close to the window so I can distinguish the nuances of the sky, and sometimes close to the table where I can hang over my books. For every ten times I move the modest furniture of my room, Lira places her things just once, and seals them in their place.

Mum?! Mum, with a mother's unique instinct, had sensed some kind of confusion that she couldn't explain, and had no way to understand. She said things time and again, and then she slipped through her daily chores as an eel slips through one's hands. Dad and Mum were as familiar as strangers to me. I thought them strangers because they did not try to touch the un-decoded world of their daughter. Even the blind hit the mark sometimes, don't they? Somewhere close they might have come. I found them familiar and close because they toiled so their "children would not miss anything," as my mum said with a clearly envious will towards life.

Since I was a child, I can remember my mother knitting magnificent sweaters for me under the light of a lamp. She knitted them with threads she took from her own sweaters. I don't know how, but with the intuition of a child who decodes the eyes of her parents, I understood that Mum's wardrobe was becoming poorer, and the wrinkles near her bright eyes were increasing while I was growing up.

My mother had—my mother has—the most beautiful face of any woman I have ever met or will meet in life. If the soul has a secret that revives it, or another soul that makes it live, then of course she is the soul for my soul. I can hardly wait for her to pass her hand through my hair and caress me, like no one else knows how, like no one else can.

Still, through that needy time to feel somebody close by, she untimely repeated that she would spare nothing for me to win the right to study.

Where could I run to? Tumult enters into a person's life from the lack of a *somebody* on whom one can lean, even just to cry, and this is not because people have everything in their hands, but because for a time, they have much to give.

You lived! Can a person wake up without a motive to dream? Or without having somebody outside of his being for whom he works? Or to whom he sends his thoughts?

On the day you left, Lira brought me this letter along with an elegant ring, the most beautiful my eyes had ever seen.

Hello Mel!

I don't know over what mountains or through which cities I will be passing while you will be pouring over these lines. I only hope . . . to still be alive.

You know what? Going away from you, I feel like I am dying inside. I didn't believe that love was so passionate, so unique. These variations of feelings for you that I am taking with me, I believed existed only in movies, in the form of a game so skillfully played, yet still a game.

But yesterday, while I had you in my arms, ahhhh . . . yesterday . . . I only recall yesterday. It brings me new energy.

If I live, I will not lose you, Mel. I want you to be the last TOUCH my hand will discover; I want you to be the last IMAGE I see in this world.

I love you so much. . .

Eri

I didn't endure any revolution inside my being, but something changed however. I started to stay up until dawn, my feet soaking in cold water to keep me awake. I flipped through my books, underlining and studying as I went. The collection of shells you had brought me from the waters of Saranda; a string of multi-shaped rocks I had taken from Valbona; dried flowers, intertwined among baskets woven by the hands of a gypsy that was fond of me; my grandmother's antique chest—these were the perfume of my life during those days. They were the most beautiful details of the world that inspired me to start fresh again under the hidden strengths of life.

Just when sleep lured me, I entered the shower. Then with a cup of coffee as my most intimate friend, I started reading again—out loud and standing in front of the fan, or lying on the floor. I was studying for . . . I was studying because, when you came back, I wanted you to find a whole differerdnt Melody. A successful, sunny, beautiful girl, who had become such . . . only for you.

Love brings out the life in Life. The Lord's love made the earth take shape. It makes the sun rise and the night fall. Magic is born when two people fall in love. What they feel makes their hearts hostage to each other. It is a part that cannot be seen, cannot be touched, but you can feel it in action; oh, more powerful than any limb of the body. With the heart that sleeps and awakens somewhere else, love is lived just to be joined to it. The footprint left in their love is without turning back, without words, unrepeatable.

Man is so different than any other creature – the Lord was humbled, humiliated, until He died on a cross, in the name of love. He left a footprint on me, a footprint that reminds me how deeply, how much, and how terribly He loves me, that He would have died just the same even only for an unworthy girl with the name of Melody Gjokaj.

I need reasons wonderfully beautiful and real, extremely deep and strong, if I am to lie down and stand up, walk and rest; reasons to live; because things don't hold me close if they are not so.

Tonight, after so much time, I know that a human being is not enough to be the only reason that keeps you alive; the only motive that makes you walk and rest. Beyond the caressing hand of my father and my mother's soft eyes, beyond the love which invaded the whole Melody, there rises a mysterious need that Life has, and without fulfilling this need, life remains incomplete. Nothing in this universe dares to replace this need.

Here it is, I successfully won the right to study. The exam results named me as one of the firsts on the list of the winners. Lira, on the other hand, was going to study law. Naturally she didn't even take the effort to open any books, or God forbid, show up for the exam. The phone calls your father made immediately guaranteed her name on the list of accepted students.

It is impossible to describe this time period in which I was a student. Such a harsh reality would only leave a shadow in these written letters; whereas the pain, the frost, the insult, the tumult, it leaves in my soul.

Just a few months after the beginning of the university year, the weapon warehouses were stormed in every corner of Albania. People changed their guns as though they were clothes on their body. They sold them, played with them, used them to congratulate on weddings, and said good morning and good night with them. The stray bullets took the life of so many people.

This monster of our country's division became crazier every day. As a girl who came from the northern lands, I felt people despising me everywhere I went. Every day this stench wafted on me.

The studios of Radio Tirana turned into a sweet shelter for me. There I calmed and let myself go there, I gave and took the best. There I endeavored for my words to calm, help, and ease somebody's anger, but deep down I knew I was just a soft voice under a mass of roars. A tiny fly rolling away under heavy winds- I was nothing more than that.

After six months of a crippled student life, the state of emergency was announced. The university closed down. Because of this, I had to separate from the only thing that brought me joy, the radio. The students abandoned their campuses, thinking that they were taking part in a short show of politics. It was different!

Eri, I could have never imagined what awaited us, not even vaguely. There were times when we passed the day in the mountains for fear that bombs might explode in the weapon warehouse near the entrance of the city.

The price of groceries had skyrocketed, but even so, you could only find them "through friends".

When we least expected them, the soldiers would raid houses to confiscate guns that were owned by almost every family. And yet, they would find nothing.

In the evening, after the chilling news reports, I slept with wet eyes and all dressed up, always ready in case the "Monster" appeared in my city; in case the shameful civil war would start.

The frightened people spoke their fears aloud, and in doing so, raised even more panic. It was like having a pot of icy soup that only appears to be boiling. Someone would hike far into the mountains; others, luckier ones, would dig for ways to cross the borders. A group of hooligans conducted our country's politics.

One face was especially hurt—the face of my city. On it, thugs dropped with fury. Every value was forgotten, everything holy was stolen, everything was crushed and walked upon. The Special Forces landed to save us, God knows who from.

"Isolate them!" the Special Forces said about us, without really putting their feet on our land. "They are savages."

This dirty game still goes on. Today they continue to treat us this way; still they 'use our hands to take chestnuts from the fire'.

The grudge and rancor in my life, the weaknesses and the lack of hope for tomorrow, after they are lived, they become alive, turn and re-turn to leave a footprint on me.

In the nights I surrendered myself to the veil of darkness. This veil brought me to you in each corner of the room, and thus leaning on you, I calmed for a bit, I calmed ... until tomorrow.

How can this body not grow weak when its heart is crippled? Isn't this world coming to an end? I wish that Tolstoy and Hugo were still alive. They would make their pens weep.

Hypocrisy flaunts success after success. Humanity wants it, looks for it, and has it. The innocent are grabbed, put in the bag of criminals, and thrown into the bottom of the sea . . . and the strangest thing is that this doesn't induce a shiver. It leaves you untouched, totally indifferent . . . because it is as fluent as the light of day coming every morning. . .

Months pass one after another while I constantly miss my favorite image, Eri's face. The image of him that I have hidden within my heart exhilarates my daylights, and turns off the sunsets. Only the mute nights understand me. They wipe my tears and put me to sleep again with that anxiety that leans as a heavy weight, a constant pain.

His silence slips from my understanding. Streams of sadness gurgle at my being while more than waiting I long for a word. In my studies, I pretend to pass my fear away. Ah yes, they pass my time. I often read even while I am eating. I have almost become a fanatic even of the moments that I breathe. I want to make the best of them, to inhale, to achieve, to have the maximum.

I live a nun's life, like in the convents where the flesh is rigorously afflicted. In my room I only sleep, and then with a pile of books and newspapers, I start for the library. Dozens of old men with glasses squint their eyes and become accustomed to my silence.

This diary I keep after midnight is the only amusement that I have. With it, I stay connected to my heart. The rest of life is simply a Must: a "Must be done".

I appear to be the classic successful student, but only I know if I really am. I feel like bursting into laughter at the students who greet and congratulate me with the whole good-behavior advertisement. Me?! Me? I don't even know who I am!

"Hey genius, take it easy," Elira's voice scratches my nerves. "There's a reason they say, 'The mind is a great thing, merry is he who doesn't have one.'"

The contrast between us is now altogether visible. Our friends are as different as our passions. There's no use talking to Lira about "my coming into this world", only by blood and soil, which leads me to the dilemma of "Why love then? Do I have a conscience simply to blacken this little life I have, only to make these days on earth harder?"

"Does a wall have ears?" my father would say. That's just how much Lira listened.

The strength of our friendship is a feeble continuity, based only on the shadow of the past. Unenthusiastically I follow her, while she fills the room with a multitude of girls who admire her, who want to become like her, with the same mischievous character and stormy laughter, with the same way to make people like her. Following the latest fashions, Lira appears transformed every week. She buys whole collections of jewelry and clothes in the most expensive stores, and harmonizes as a charming female or a spoiled muse. Under the silky mix of colored hair and skin shining from the fluids of creams, with masks that change according to timetables, deep in those wide, dark eyes, hides the Lira that sleeps when she pleases, sometimes during the day, and sometimes during the night. She is as amused as in the ecstasy of a holiday season.

Sometimes we happen to talk of the past, being careful that the name Ermal is not touched, as a rotten string of thread that rips within a blink. Maybe this is the only thing I can't forgive Lira about—she never once encouraged me to weep on her shoulders or even sigh in her presence. Nevertheless, amid the drowsiness of the night, she comes close to me, and zealously tells me in detail what new things are happening in her life.

Here Comes Aldo

I met Aldo in the office of the radio's chief editor while we were discussing the new structure of my radio show. His father was one of the few people who encouraged my new ideas and the only one who did not hesitate to give them life. A multitude of well-known radio producers pushed me to articulate only their sounds, to always quote their often dry sentences.

Every feature in Aldo gives expression to a uniqueness that is totally disliked by many.

"Wow, you're the young lady hosting 'Through the eyes of youth'? It is an honor for me," he said, as his father introduced us. "I have heard that your show is very popular."

Immediately after that, he sunk into the couch. Meanwhile, I asked permission to continue with my work at another time.

"I notice my presence confuses you, young lady," he said, while I began gathering CDs, newspapers, and a number of papers. "I would never allow myself to become a barrier to the rhythmic life of this radio, so, with your permission, I will go." With two steps, he hopped outside like a frog.

His father did not comment on the lack of courtesy of his prodigal progeny, as I would later learn. Meanwhile, my mind replayed the words that had been clothed with a gibe.

Aldo studied singing and played the guitar. Almost all his wardrobe was made of dark black clothes that contrasted with his long, yellow hair let loose on his shoulders. On his shoulder, there was the tattoo of a snake with its tongue out, spitting poison. These and many other things, obliged one to think, "What is this species?" He was comfortable in the center of a group of youngsters, but he was also a mediator of solitude.

And he was so handsome. Aldo had a beauty that required time to uncover from his many metallic accessories.

I was leaving in an irritated mood when I met him again. Sitting on the stairs where the whole arsenal of radio employees steps, he immediately stood up, letting me know he had been waiting for me.

"You're finished? I waited to say that it would be an enormous pleasure for me, if one day we could go out together, just for a drink. I am aware that you must have a busy agenda, but if you created a tiny space to relax, it might be worthwhile. I give you my word that I will make you change your mind from thinking you have met an alien today.

"That is very kind of you, but it is as you said, I am very busy. Nevertheless, could you tell me something out of curiosity, please? Who told you this is the impression I had of you?" I turned to him, exultant that I had the chance for a little revenge.

"Oh, you are not the first to think that, but let's say that it can be read quite clearly in the transparency of those sky-blue eyes," he responded immediately, while he courteously let me pass.

After that day, I saw him "sprout out" everywhere around me. Aldo became the most systematic member of the library, challenging even me. Those days also revived in him the passion for lectures of Albanian language and literature. He even took notes regularly, and, supposedly out of coincidence, he always had something to do at the radio station every time I recorded and selected materials for my program. Not to mention that he liked the menu of the restaurant where I ate so much that he could be found there even in the mornings. Anyway, for the first time, this ever-growing friendship blazed a kind of pleasure that had abandoned me since the last time I saw you, Eri.

Evening conversation with him made me look forward to the sunset and the time when he whistled "Wind of Change" under my balcony.

Elira had an instant aversion to Aldo, and she showed this with some whispered words.

As a tactful girl, she was careful not to go against me, even though in the first opportunity she had to be alone with him, she emptied on him all the rancor she had been conserved with time and care.

According to her, Aldo was in vain going after Melody, because she was madly in love with her cousin who was studying in America. Even children in our town knew that they were meant for each other.

One night, when I was going out for dinner with Aldo, she decided to ask me:

"You know that it is not in my nature to mind the business of others, and naturally I would not interfere with your decisions either, Melody, but I am giving myself the right to ask you— has something changed toward Ermal?"

This hit like lightning! In two years, this was the first time Lira mentioned your name. I felt the blood coming up to my face in anger. I lost against the temptation to make fun of those two wrinkles that formed near her eyebrows during those rare moments when she looked serious.

"You might know the answer better than I do. Actually, it would be honest of you, according to what you call friendship, to tell me," I faced her angrily.

"Nonsense!" she mumbled. But when she met my angry sight, she added, "You pretend that I would keep such a thing hidden, when there is nothing among my most intimate thoughts that I haven't shared with you?"

I was convinced about this, but I remained convinced without admitting it to her. It wasn't worth going further. However, silence is often worse than speaking. Silence builds its own cell and tortures your meditations there inside, while speaking leads you to the key, through which you may even feel more redeemed. I looked at her reproachfully, right into those beautiful eyes, and I left with a calmness that was so only in appearance.

Aldo, together with two of his friends, owned one of the most frequented discos in the capital.

There I managed to know him a little bit better. He stimulated me to feel like a princess.

"Mel, how are you? Do you feel comfortable? Do you need anything? Hey, how do you like this music? Are you tired, do you want to rest? When you want to leave, just give me a signal,"— and thousands of other offers. He treated me as if everything around us, peeping or ceasing, speaking or silent, lived only for me. It was everything a woman deserves, expects, and dreams about.

But when he danced in the circle of his half naked friends, he resembled a beast. It looked like the distorted sounds of heavy-metal music, its rhythm and pulse, posses and electrify him in a manner that I was neither familiar with, nor did I like.

My roommate, Dana, constantly urged me to pursue in Aldo more than our current friendship.

"How pleasant! Oh, he is amazing," she commented, walking carelessly around the room. She tried to persuade me to see that beyond the conversations, which seemed friendly, he hid his pretext to be close to Mel as a girl. And this *was* the reality!

It wasn't a coincidence that his eyes shined when he came close to me. How strange that he, who did not esteem any human, was nervous when I looked at him. My word and judgment concerned him. It caressed my pride, as it would for anyone, but nothing more.

We danced, not long after a lengthy conversation I had with Dana, in which she and I agreed to reject her suspicion as being totally misunderstood, even absurd.

It was one of those songs in which the background doesn't offer more than the touch and respiration of the person close to you, and while Aldo kept his hands on my back, he was shaking.

"Melody, every beautiful quotation that I read or hear," he whispered, "every rhythm that I dance, while I close my eyes and sleep, if I don't think about you, I am poor and without life. I am bewitched by you . . . by your passion to pour yourself even into the most ordinary things; I am wholly passionate about this feminine fragility that gives you so much charm. Please do not deny me this happiness. I swear this is the first time in my life I feel this way. I want to ask you just to leave reasoning out of this; to let yourself be free!

(Why should I not enjoy this history?

How do you dare allow this to cross your mind, when somebody else owns your heart?

Who says this?! You are reduced to a fool who cannot even control herself.

Alright, alright, as you wish. You are always right.

No, I really mean it, let's think this through. Who knows, maybe I will forget that person. Afterwards, there is no sign to show that he still feels for me. Perhaps he can hardly remember my name, while I stay here and worship him as some people do in a temple.)

Oriented by his arms, I woke up from debating with myself.

"Aldo, this is very pleasant to hear. And I would never want to hurt you," I replied, concerned by his apologizing look and nervous breath, "but I can't give you something that I don't own anymore. And, if carelessly I have given you any reason to think there is something between us, I deeply apologize."

He forged a smile and then said, "Mel, it is such a fortune to meet you, to find you, to have you. I cannot understand how a guy can treat a girl like you the way that fellow Ermal has done. And I am not saying this only because I feel so strongly for you, but because I see you are isolated from the world. However things might be, you have at least the right to know. Even if he is the perfect one, fallen from heaven, compared to you, he is just a child—a less than mediocre boy."

"Aldo, this is not my problem. I have promised him that I will wait. See? I wear his ring on my finger. But believe me, it is not a matter of promise at all, or some kind of obligation that must be respected. This has nothing to do with it. The thing is, I . . . I love Eri. I can remove him neither from the day, nor the night; not from the most ordinary moments, or the most special ones. Even if I wanted to, I could not do it. And this is not his fault. Maybe with his prolonged silence, he has already given me that blessed answer, but I am still too weak to accept it."

"How can you know, Mel? You have deprived yourself of the opportunity to love again. You treat this as a crime. Here, let's consider my case, to be concrete. Why won't you try to look at me differently than just a friend?"

"Hey, do you want to be hurt at any cost?" I turned with a tone of affection and also reproach, "Do you think I would allow myself to experiment by using you; by abusing your feelings?! I don't have a way to let you know how important your friendship is to me, but please know that it is very dear to my heart. If you haven't noticed, you are the only friend that I have here; the only person whom I could follow with my eyes closed, wherever you led me."

"But Mel, you can't deny that you have to wake up from this world you have built," he insisted, "so allow me to be the one that is close to you. Let's simply try it, Mel. You have nothing to lose."

But these deceitful pleads did not impress me!

"Let's try?! Try what? I might be insane, but I will wait, without wandering on caprices that send me where my heart is not," I said, leaving in the middle of the dance.

The immovable Mel was alone in the flow of waiting.

I was stopped in time; ever more stubborn to those who surrounded me, ever more tender-hearted to what frightened me. Seating on the railroad of waiting, I couldn't stop the seasons from changing colors, even though I really wanted to.

Dana, as if giving lectures in a course on the perils of memories, repeated that I was living my life based on a teenager's caprices. She too believed I was killing the opportunity to be free, to love again.

Despite all these things, I believed... I wanted to believe that love triumphs over time, triumphs over blood feud, and that it disdains egoism. However it was, I despised everybody's opinion, mainly because I feared they were right. Solitude had reduced me to act like an old woman who fanatically guards her most precious memory and, whether she realizes it or not, everything else is made unimportant in her eyes.

What drew me to hope, or be deceived, was the faith I still had in the same sparkling eyes that I could distinguish within me every time I remembered you. Didn't the same thing happen to you?!

After that night, I didn't spend any more time with Aldo, until he later appeared during one of the hardest times of my life.

Aldo was guzzling alcohol night and day. He was more exalted, more energetic, and more sincere than ever, and he kept coming under my balcony, where Dana waited for him. She cared for him with sisterly care, and heard the outbursts of his angry caprices.

As she entered the room, Dana poured onto me the heat of her fear for him, accusing me of being 'heartless'. However, my conscience did not burden any corner of my heart.

I don't know how, I don't know why, but not one sight of him ever traveled deeper than my eyes.

Rogues Attacking

This morning I enjoyed waking up when the light had not yet come down through the hills, and the air was still fresh. Two rays of light were resting on top of the two hills in front of me, and everywhere around them the shadowy darkness still ruled. The morning enticed peace all around; whereas the afternoons in front of my balcony lit the sky. This place reddens from the radiance of the soft clouds over the lake. The water sparkles, the cliffs shine bright with sunlight, unable to touch the nuances of the sky.

How beautifully the doors of the day are closed by our country's colors, as if they didn't want to importune anyone.

The fire in the sky dies. The background serves two mountains close to each other, untouched, undisturbed, painted by the brush of Him who poured out with "favoritism" the graces of this land. It is a luxury for the soul to live in this place.

Each and every day of my life, I would like to take my breaths here, always here, evermore here; the sunsets I would place near the gladiolas, around the fields and woods, there where flowers spread like islands in the midst of vast waters.

You know, Eri, that I am simply writing contours, faded contours of landscapes whose beauty cannot be described by words. The only thing one can do is let their beauty shine within one's soul. Divinely my place communicates with me. Never has its beauty been simply ordinary to me.

Time has brought peace to most of the cities, but it has unnerved ours. Strolls in the streets have died because people fear stray bullets. The voices of children are also gone. Every time I come home, I find another neighbor moving, another empty apartment.
The remaining inhabitants practice the 'sport' of breaking windows and crashing bricks. The Kikaj hooligans are getting stronger in fame and power.

Skënder still holds the position of mayor of the city, violating the law he represents. They are the law and the privilege. They use the law as a personal privilege. Those who couldn't even finish high school serve as today's "justice", with their enviable diplomas and CVs.

If they like something, they make it theirs. If they envy a post, they take it. They wait you in and they walk you out, they intrigue and they judge, they hurt and they humiliate, they wound and they eliminate, and, of course, for each case they also execute the "guilty" ones. They kill you first and then they weep for you; they massacre you and then they mourn you; they dig your grave and then they are the first in line to comfort your family.

When the charming progeny of the Kikaj put their eye on a girl, they devoured her.
Dozens of teen girls have been dragged through the city lanes, violated and disabled by them. Naturally, in the end, they brought these poor girls back to their families so they could cure them.

The people drop their gaze in front of them, hide their daughters and change their way, praying never to meet them. The terror of the Kikaj name rests under every roof.

Though Lira knew no fear or tutelage, learning of these things from her hometown, while living in a totally indifferent environment, made her hatred for the Kikaj even more consuming. It brought her down with new anxiety, anxiety for her uncle, for Diti, and for her mother. It didn't even enter her mind to fear for herself, because Elira was strong and secure. Daring and exploding in every movement and expression, in every word or mimic, she was a person who would never give up or surrender.

But . . . it happened one rainy night in February that a deranged voice called out for her. It was late, so I stood up to accompany her, like I always did in late hours. We were aware of the fact that the times during which we had the misfortune to be students were dreadful times.

She caressed my hair.

"Hey, go on with studying. I have no idea who it is, but whoever it is, I am not going to stay long. I'm exhausted," she said, closing the door lightly after herself.

A feeling of homesickness had invaded her lately; some kind of apathy that the elderly call, without hesitance, a "bad premonition".

Sleepily she went downstairs until . . .

I would write limitless ellipses and infinite dots just to avoid what my words will tell: each conviction with pleasure I would take as a life sentence, if I could only change this truth that cuts the very depths of my heart.

Sleepily Lira went downstairs, only to be found hidden behind a building, unconscious.

We all have cases when we would like to turn back time, right? And do things differently! To make wiser choices! If I had gone downstairs with Lir
a, maybe . . . maybe nothing would have happened to her. Or would I have suffered the same fate, too? Maybe not? Maybe Lira would have escaped the claws of those who have long forgotten their humanity.

I will never know how things would have gone, but after that night, a merciless reproach has accused and punished me thousands of times.

I waited more than an hour reading, then two, and then I worried and I awakened Dana. We went outside and checked all of the benches near the dorms. Except for some dogs that angrily barked, nobody seemed to be awake.

"This girl makes me crazy," I complained to Dana, while we returned to our room, still angry.

"At least she could have called from downstairs. It wouldn't have cost her a thing," Dana approved.

However, a feeling of a heinous omen had grasped me. Could that have been her cry while she was being beaten like a small, unprotected animal?

Could someone's sleep have been interrupted while she was begging for mercy; while she was being humiliated and forever ruined?

While I continued reading, the strong men of the Kikaj grinned next to Lira, those rogues who had come down the mountain lanes in their official cars.

"Something has happened to her," I pulled Dana, who had just gotten in bed. "Surely something has happened to her."

"We will go to the police district," I added while throwing her a sweater to wear.

"All this is very odd, very scary," I spoke to myself more than to Dana. "I can't remember a case in which she has left in such a way, without notice, without leaving an address."

With a very weak voice, Dana reminded me that Lira would never forgive me if I was serious about the idea of reporting to the police.

Anyway, I didn't doubt for a moment, because that delicate voice convinced me that . . . *that the night was covering her cries; the rain was washing away her blood*?!

How can I ever forget that body that had been damaged and made fragile within a few hours, that small body coiled in a dirty blanket while it fled toward the hospital in the police car?

I don't know how Aldo came to know, I don't know how he arrived there. I know that he appeared there within minutes after I was told that my friend was found half-alive at the edge of the campus.

While Lira was surrounded by doctors, Aldo softly put me under his arms saying, "These tears you are now shedding are a privilege that you can't recognize. Lira can hear you; she can feel your presence. Your words should awake in her the desire for life. It will be fine, my sweetheart. Ok? Will you keep this in your mind? Come on. Everything with be fine."

Of course, his soft hands, while they kept me within his reach, not only caressed my face and body, but also the pulse of life itself. I don't know how I could have continued if those words had been missing.

Immediately he called the families, and through a network of friends he assured that the doctors would do their best for a dormitory student who didn't have any relatives nearby. He took care that the buzzing journalists would not make a fuss about the name of the student violated in the middle of the night.

On the thresholds of those moments, when everything turned upside-down in front of me, I forgot everything; I stopped living for anybody, including myself, and I remember I only breathed so that Lira could live once more. Just once more! I turned my eyes toward Him on Who we turn at the end of every road, when we haven't left a path untried or a place without crashing. Like the feverish and woeful song of a hopeless person, I begged the Omnipresent to keep Lira alive for me.

"If you exist, whoever you are, please save her," I sobbed. "I beg you, do it for me—for my sake."

How could I know that one day, the Omnipresent, who sometimes seemed "heartless", would become my most beautiful joy? When I would lose all my friends, He would be there, a Friend, a Comforter, a Hope, all for me. Today, not even the flesh of my body is closer to me than He is. He is the Light I can't wait to see . . . the Spirit of my life.

"You must, you must to save her," I mumbled like an insane creature.

I didn't know what to do! What in the world could I do? Like that time when Flavio, forgotten by friends, afraid about tomorrow, bid me farewell; like that time when I wandered in the question: "What if Eri doesn't come back?" Life there inside me rustled like a soft breeze.
"Nothing, you can do . . . absolutely nothing."

Just as the doctors assured me that any progress or backward turn was in Elira's hands, I went into her room. Knowing me, you will understand that whenever I am in a hospital, I melt, even if nobody I know is a patient there. Just the way I was, like a frightened child, I continued crying over her bed. Hoping she would hear my soft voice, I kept whispering to her ear: "Don't fear, Lira. Don't be afraid, sweetheart, don't be afraid any longer. Nobody will hurt you. I will be close to you when you wake up."

"Please, please Lira, get better. Think about your uncle. He must not see you in this condition!"

In that narrow room that smelled of sweat and medicine, everything, from the walls to the bed, seemed completely unclean, filthy.

I breathed slowly, I wept fast. Confused as I was, I imagined scenes and created images and moments which would fit the wild reality . . . as I would learn later on.

Around the afternoon, a little before her parents arrived, Lira started waking. She moved her eyelids slowly. I have never been happier than when I saw those tired eyes focus on me. She stayed that way for some moments and then it seemed as if she tried to speak. Yes, she was trying to say something. She started saying that horrible something, that introduced me to the depths of hate.

"Flavio's cou . . . sins, they . . . were . . . they. . . "

All that Lira articulated, all that would remain on her lips on that horrible night, was this. Never again would she add anything to these words.

She buried her thoughts on that dirty bed, also burying with them the Lira we had once known… long ago.

Your aunt, with the same dynamic temperament as her daughter, exhausted every method to pull out the names or the faces of the violators, without the tiniest achievement. She would wake her up in the middle of the night to ask her, she would cry in front of her, heartbroken, to arouse some mercy, she would frequent psychologists, fortune tellers, and yet she would only understand when Lira would face them in the midst of hundreds of people and hide behind her father, howling for help.

I loved, no, no, I didn't love; I was enchanted by the dream to see those people hanged, while they were in pain and crying for mercy next to each other. I understood that yet for a long time, this would remain only a dream. Who could touch them? What threatened them? They didn't mind setting a school on fire if a small Kikaj were threatened in a fight of peers.

A dormitory student who met Lira at the gate had told her that people were waiting for her, further down. With heavy eyelids, without caring why she had to go further down, Lira went down the stairs and, with that unconcerned walk of hers, she had left behind the dorm cafeteria. Nonetheless, once they saw her, it was too late for her to turn back, horribly late.

They covered her mouth with a towel and dragged her through the street, starting a spectacle that would make even an animal cry. Beating and violating her, they enjoyed her suffering, they got drunk with her groans, and they strengthened themselves with female fragility.

Lira had confirmed the doubts with which they had come; she confessed that you and Ruby were not in Albania, that her uncle was still isolated in his house, and that soon he would join his sons.

"Let's let her live to mourn the death of her uncle," they greeted her at last, leaving her half-naked in the darkness of that morning of crippled hopes.

But this was a job for them; one of the many jobs they start with passion and finish without desire; that they design slowly and put into action quickly. Nevertheless, they had to go back to their unfortunate hometown during the night. At dawn, they had to be present to serve as law-enforcement in that city which fate had cursed with them

As any brother would share with his sister, as he would melt and pour himself out in front of her, not minding to show his weakness, Flavio sobbed like a child while he was telling me all this. Wanting him to rejoice in their revenge party, his cousins had been eager to boost his morale: "Hey, cousin, we fixed the case of the niece," he had heard on the telephone. Naturally he had perfectly understood the meaning of these words. Who knew better than him how their cousins fixed things? That's why he had immediately come back to Albania.

As he arrived home, they had confessed to him how they had crippled Lira. Laughing like hungry beasts, they had told him how they had soiled the fragile body of the one he loved, how she begged for mercy; how, just as a souvenir of that night, they had lined her lips with a knife; how she would never live the female dream of being a mother.

"Look at me well," Flavio had replied, "because this is the last time. From today on, I am dead to you."

In a laughter that has remained unthreatened to this very day, they had continued:
"We had never considered you among the living."

He swore never again to step on the bloody land, made messy by those inhuman filths that were his cousins. He left Albania, crying even more than he did three years ago, and returned to the new, empty house, without anyone he loved, without anyone he hated.

He held me and hugged tightly, without forgetting to remind me that at his house I always had a place to stay, and that in him I had an understanding friend, a brother to lean on. I felt much fear for him. I feel much fear for him, just like I do for you, Eri; fear about a foggy tomorrow of uncertainties.

Losing Lira

I didn't tell Flavio that my friendship with Lira was breaking. I saw how she painted pretense on her faded face. Her silence on the name Ermal had already hurt our friendship, and now Lira had rapidly changed from an unstoppable girl to a sulky one.

Elira ignored what had happened to her. Though I tried with all I could to make her talk to me, she pretended not to remember anything. She would hide her look, fake a smile and add:
"No, nothing, I don't remember anything."
But I happened to know that memory cannot erase such a terrible mark from somebody's soul.

[*I say I happened to know, because there was a dream that used to torment my sleep also.
I see that dream when I sleep; I see it when I wake up. I am reminded of it when I'm hanging with friends, and I often remember it when I am alone.*]

The dream pictures a little girl. She goes to her neighbor's apartment, a tender old man who comes and goes from her house as though it is his own. This time, I don't know why, the old man grins like a monster that has smelled a prey. He takes her by the hand, and lays her on a couch that is rotten just like him.

The dream becomes a nightmare. A huge beast pleases its instincts. And she, night after night, year after year, awakes in the middle of the night, yelling:
"Please, please, don't!"

She kept hiding and writhing under the table in her room, wanting to escape, only to forget. But still she came out of there, always terrified.

And this has carved my character into that of a scared bird. Dozens of times I thought I was ready to share this with you, Eri. Many times I left home to come and share my crushing secret with you, only to delay it for another day.

But when we separated, and while I was waiting for you, this wound kept scratching me harder, because people are inclined to bring back the anxiety of all incidents at once. We are prone to meditate on the diversity of our life's cruelties. Or maybe this is just me?

It seems that sad events are unfolding one after the other, right Eri?! It's all right. The hardship was to live through them, because after such things happen to us, after these things that cripple or break us, life is hidden. In every moment, life is ready, it eagerly waits, and it loves to give us a hand to raise us up. Believe me; it has done this for me. Just as sand paper cleans away rust, life has set me free from the power that enticed self-guilt and self-pity, from the fences I put up to live in isolation.

But let's go back to Elira.

She needed to speak, to cry, to writhe, and to crash. If in the middle of the night when she woke up to seek help, when she lifted her eyelids, I wanted her to see that I was there next to her. If she turned off the light, and broke into tears or stuttered with herself, I wanted her to feel that someone was close to her. Of course, no one ever mentioned her studies in law. As for me, during the exam season, I would go to Tirana and take my exam, and the next afternoon I would be back again at Lira's house.

But one day when I came back, I found her engaged to be married.
How did I feel?? How should I have felt?! Startled?! Shocked?! Little considered?! Despised?! Unappreciated?! All of these sensations invaded me while Lira followed my reaction very attentively.

I congratulated her as formality requires. Could I make those eyes answer my questions?

How could I? They were no more than two dark inns, wherein was hidden everything that wanted life, every signal that wanted to live. Where could I borrow some courage, just a little bit, so as to grab her and shake her hard? In the sleepless nights of our dreams?! No, I didn't find the strength to ask her, or reproach her. I didn't say or do anything disastrous.

Isn't it weird that a person who endures, let's say, an unpleasant surprise, just melts? He cannot find the strength to somehow swallow the shock, or to recover and react.

I continued going to Elira's house brokenhearted. But now, while I followed her through the rooms, she kept showing me the concise needle-point of the carpets and tapestry, the elegant models of lace and a dozen tablecloths, sheets, curtains, and plenty of rugs to inaugurate a handcraft shop. Her mother had crafted these things since her childhood, with the hope of a happier marriage.

People murmured quietly, but loudly they stated that Lira was lucky, and "nobody" doubted that she wouldn't be a wife on scythe seventh heaven of happiness. She would travel the world alongside this well-to-do, middle-aged man, whose features were still graceful, and who came from a well-respected family! She didn't walk very gracefully or with dashing feminine refinement on her wedding day; she didn't shine in those moments that every girl dreams of, nor did she greet anyone on her way to the altar, where a good man was waiting for her.

Now, yes, I had lost Elira.

Striving to Live

I am holding my spirit in my hands, but my hands are fragile like spider webs. My life is only a scribble on these pages!

Surely there is no cure, no talent, or genius to cure pain. It only shrivels your heart; it kills all your energies, your desires, your life.

I feel like I am no longer living. I am like flesh without life. But unfortunately, I can still feel. Strength, I have not—meaning I cannot find—everything passes close to me, softer than a breeze that barely touches you. Nothing gives strength to my arms, or to my mind to make her desire participating in the flow of life.

Ah, I wish my soul had never gone through this numbed state! I do not know what to think, let alone what to write. In the mornings I wish I had never been born; in the nights, I wish I'd never wake up.

With a gentle persistence, Aldo comes to me every day. Like a good brother, he passes his hand through my hair and hears my outbursts of sadness. Like a friend, he outlines my occasional smile; like a true partner he investigates my unspoken thoughts. He takes me by the hand, leading me through the lecture halls; he leads me to the radio studios, turning practically into a co-worker for me. He separates me from loneliness, and serves me with the most romantic surprises.

And naturally, he doesn't forget to invite me into the depths of his loving feelings. Jealously, he strives to be everywhere around me. I obey. I obey like a beaten child, who sees even the palm of a monster to be an angelic touch; but Aldo invests his heart. Nevertheless, his fervor is lukewarm to me. How is it possible that the heart longs after only one person? How is it possible that my will to be free from Eri always remains a dream for tomorrow?

Eri, today I desired you close to me, in a stronger, special way. My third volume of poetry was published. The most capricious professors, the editor, and even the critics congratulated me. Some professors appeared enthusiastic for my talent's imprint on Albanian letters.
I have heard that professor Engjëll is living in France. I always enjoyed sharing my emotions with him.

I so wanted to make you happy, too, sweetheart . . . but . . .

I am in my room. I am eating, and at the same time, I am stopping to write. Lately I have been hurriedly abandoning the lecture halls to go to "The Office of Blood-Feud Reconciliation". Interestingly enough, I was the first female to seek membership in this organization.

Yesterday the office was filled with village chiefs from northern Albania. What wisdom can be found in the lips of our elderly!

A week ago, an old blood feud was reconciled. This made me happy. I almost thought I was helping Eri. I felt like I was doing something for him.

And yet, between the comfort of this office and the hopeless cry of the people locked in their houses, there stands a huge mountain.

Dana doesn't understand how my feelings interlock and loosen, stop and fall, why they die and live just for Ermal. I cannot say that I do…

I wander around in my room, trying to find something to do. I try to forget for a little while, and then I turn back there, to the same place, to the same name. I turn back to the name of Ermal Korinaj. He cannot be anything more than he already is- the center of my universe.

I fear that I expect more from his heart than it wants to give. This, only this, would challenge, defeat, and humble me.

Aldo continues to be my silhouette.

When you put your heart in a person, and then you see he isn't where you desire him to be, you break into pieces; yet surprisingly, without understanding, you still love him dearly.

It seems that my fate is entangled somewhere in the fog of time. It is hidden where I cannot see, where I cannot find the path.

The Death of a Good Man

"Mel, the phone was for you. They will call you again in five minutes," said Dana, just coming in the room that evening. "Did they say who?" I asked.

"A guy from Ahhhhhmerica," she emphasized "ah", laughing noisily.
"Oooh, you're so mean!" I said, and went out of the room to go down to the first floor where the dormitory's phone was.

"Mel," I recognized my mom's thundering voice on the phone, "How's my daughter?"
Without waiting for an answer, she added:
"Unfortunately I have something sad to tell you."
"What . . . what has happened?" I asked, and my knees started to tremble.
"They shot Lira's uncle. He's dead. Today at. . . Mel, are you still there? Melody, do you hear me?"

I dropped the phone with a spirit that made my body tremble and shocked my mind.
Wherever I turned, these sounds followed me: he's dead, he's dead, he's dead.

Endless crowds of people were comforting each other around that yard, in that amazing decor of flowers and trees.

If there's a moment that unites violent and peaceful people, those who hate strongly and those who hate less, those who believe in God and those who have no God, that is death. Death humbles them, death horrifies them; it touches even the iciest spirit, making it feel a trace of the fact that its adversary is not another human; its enemy is not one who doesn't share the same ideas. The enemy is someone else; someone who seems a fairy tale character to us, a fairy tale that gives us strength to destroy each other. Our enemy is the evil, the malign, the deceptive, the devil, or whatever we name it. And no matter how ridiculous it may look to us, he is the one who hides, the one who reduces our lives to a mishmash of feelings and hatred. He is the one who hides behind so-called morals and the 'Kanun'; he slithers behind principles and laws, amidst families and neighborhoods, in little towns and big cities.

I don't care, Eri, if it sounds old, if this comes as an antique thing in your ears or anyone else's. Today I only bow down to one thing . . . and that is the Truth.

Some fragments of the funeral, some pieces that I will write about have remained with me. They will never be detached from what I am and from what I will be tomorrow. They flash before my eyes whenever they want, without asking or considering me, making my heart ache each time they come.

Close to the coffin, in a dark suit, like a pale jewel, with no feelings, with no red eyes or wet cheeks, there stood your brother Diti. Holding out his hand as the head of the funeral, he on whom the eyes of the crowd focused with pity and respect, Diti gave answers and thanks. Time after time, as if pushed by an instinct, he turned toward his mother, caressed her hair and hands, and whispered something to her. Diti made people feel compassion even if they had never known compassion.

Alongside him, stately as always, in a shiny dark suit and starched collar, Luan Korinaj leaned lifelessly.

According to tradition, when a blood feud has a chance to end, and perhaps life starts the cure of forgetting, the Kikaj sought the so-called 'word of honor', to be at the funeral. This gave them a guarantee—an assurance that no unpleasant surprise would happen during the funeral. Together with his relatives, Flavio's father met the long line of men, repeating consolation formulas.

It was exactly then when Lira's well-sheltered secret would become stronger than her. It would crawl out of Elira herself, and leave her standing there alone.

Right when her eyes met Shpëtim's, Flavio's cousin, she started groaning and stepping backwards slowly, as though she had seen a ghost. She walked backwards, slipped, fell, until crashing onto her father. Without looking, Lira hid behind him, mumbling:
"Them. Him, him. Dad, it's him. Help . . . help, help me."

I swear, Eri, you would think that her whole spirit would separate from her body right there.
Her father, looking in the direction of his daughter, was terrified, and appeared to understand what he had tried so hard to discover. He turned totally towards her, hugged her body and hid her on his chest, covering her head with his hands, as though he wanted to take her wholly inside himself, just to hide her from those who might hurt her.

All eyes froze on them. What on earth would be needed to melt this arsenal of eyelids which had learned to see only beyond their own noses?

Exactly at this time, out of nowhere, Diti appeared. Diti stopped in front of Flavio's father and the men who followed him, to impede their progress towards the coffin—there where women mourned, where pain was freer, truer. With the calmness of a diplomat, he stayed in front of them, without a stir in his look. An innocent look, and yet horrible. Even one whose desire was to kill or feared no human being would have trembled in front of him. Diti stood like an angel in front of those who don't even know the meaning of purity, but still dread it. He didn't need to say anything. Judgment and pain, disdain, dignity, and distance: all were there in his eyes.

And the Kikaj backed out. They turned "with dignity" to let it be understood they respected the sadness of these people, nevertheless . . . ohh, they were all right. In the end, they had only avenged their grandfather, whose grave they didn't even remember.

Oh, Eri, can you see?! Can you penetrate beyond that? Do you understand what thin veil joins you to these people?! What edifice separates you, sweetheart, from their evil minds?! They neglect and kill the beautiful voice of conscience; they bow down to their beastly instinct wherever and whenever they smell it.

Surely this pain will hurt you for a long time! It has all rights to do so, doesn't it?!

Eri, I don't know if there is anything under heaven to give you the strength to go ahead, but if there is, I know it is not blood feud; so please do not look for healing there.

You would be deceived!

Diti listened to the speeches of friends who had disappeared in time of need, and now they spoke like heroes in front of the crowd. Untouched by their words, uninvolved in the cry of neighbors, he threw a fist of dirt on the coffin like many others did. He looked like a distant, deeply hidden iceberg.

When the crowd started to disperse, he sat on top of his father's new house.

Lord, this is the peak of human tragedy. Nothing and no one can rip out hope deeper than this moment can. This moment tears your life with its claws right before your eyes; it covers all tomorrows in darkness, and you have no desire left to care about living. You go among the graves with a corpse that, even though it doesn't talk, walk, or live anymore, still is a part of your beloved person— the body of whom you once touched, and you must then, after having thrown it into a hole, turn back, turn back without him, turn back defeated, turn back empty. There is no other time in this life when a person can touch the peak of suffering in his spirit, the pinnacle of the desire not to be, not to exist.

Totally indifferent to greeting anyone, he then started throwing small rocks from the fresh dirt of the grave. With a sad curiosity, people turned, even as they started leaving, to follow his reactions.

"Let's go, my dear, we will come again tomorrow," Elira's mum caressed him, "See, he is here now, forever. Only for us."

With his eyes fixed on the grave, he didn't move at all.

When a person finds himself here, in a place like this, it seems that even if the whole world fell in front of you, you would not be tempted to lower your eyes and look at it; that's how cold the cut of pain leaves you. Nevertheless, sooner or later there are some small pieces in the human heart that always come and carefully steal the attention away from the pain.

My attention was on Diti.

With a shaky courage, I separated from my parents and went close to him.
"Do you want to stay alone with your dad?" I whispered close to his ear. He stayed like that for a little while, and then moved his head, approving.
"Hey, Eri would feel better if I accompanied you," I spoke again in a low voice. These words made our special bond, this was our big secret. He slowly looked at me like that lamb of three

years ago, when everything had just started, and again he approved softly with a nod of his head. The people were scattered, and the twilight that hurried to take over those graves terrified me.

With an elegant care, Diti moved the wreaths of flowers from the tombstone, reading all the names, condolences, and lines written on them, one after the other. Then he started talking as if his father was sitting there in front, with his face leaning on his hands and listening . . .

"What will I do now? You had found the way to reconcile, right, Dad? Didn't you say so? You promised you would return from the Kikaj's home. You would return free . . . You knew, Daddy . . . and you didn't tell me? Why didn't you tell me?"

"Diti, look at me for a few seconds," I said and went closer to him. "If you feel like crying, that doesn't mean you are weak. We all need to do something at the point of such despair, and tears are often the only way to make us feel better."

"I don't want to feel better," he turned to me in an explosive and accusing tone, as if I had asked something dishonorable, although he leaned his head on one shoulder, and I saw tears in his eyes. Little cataracts silently fell down his cheeks. Sobbing, he fell into my arms and put his head on my shoulder. An angel had chosen my arms to lean on, to trust, to pour out his sadness and tears, causing me to feel completely new sensations, pure, divine sensations.

On my shoulder there mourned a child whose father lied fresh under the dirt, "in the name of honor". Where could I find, where could I turn for words of solace? Are there any?! I don't even dare to search.

When I was a teenager like him, I had lost an old wrinkled woman who had caressed me, cradled, bathed, and lulled me. I had roamed the house and walked the streets in her fragile arms, I drank from the same cup that she drank, I ate from her plate; she warmed me with the love that is unique of a grandmother for the child of her own child. From the window of our apartment, we watched the messy world run. She knew how to make the big world small and beautiful to me. My granny was the first to confront me with death. While standing in front of those breathless nostrils, I cried with all the strength I had, because the softest person, the best, my closest and dearest friend was no longer talking to me, was not answering me, and was not waking up. But I had not been there when she closed her eyes for the last time, as Diti had seen his father do. My grandmother had not been deformed in my sight.

"I cannot do a thing, Mel. Not a thing. I can't go back home. I don't want to. Dad also is alone. How can I live . . . not seeing him? Who will I talk to now, who will I sleep with, who will read to me? Only yesterday he touched Eri's and Rubin's books, smelled their clothes, kissed their names embroidered on their pillows; he even found the picture of a girl that Eri had left under his pillow.

Of course, everything is reversible, apart from death, Eri. Everything has a tomorrow, everything invents a way out, except death; but I would be insincere if I said that these words didn't agitate me.

So this is how things stood! Could it be clearer than that?! And wasn't this the perfect time?! Who was she? How was that possible?

Praise God that Diti didn't let me meditate on all the faces of the girls I knew in order to guess who she might have been.

"It was your picture, Mel," he added.

"When the first shot was heard, I was inside. Immediately after that, I heard my dad scream. I had never heard him scream like that. He was telling me not to go outside. Even then, he was thinking of me. Right after that, another shot was heard, and then another one . . . I can't remember how many. But what I will never forget is . . . my daddy . . . on the ground . . . with his stomach torn apart. He was swimming . . . in blood. I ran and leaned him onto my lap. He tried to reach his hand... toward my face, tried to laugh, and said to me:
'Shhhh, my life, you are free now; you will play, you will go to school. Haven't you been missing these things?' 'I haven't been missing a thing, I swear Daddy,' I said to him, crying.
He passed his hand through my hair, looked at me slowly, and with tears remaining in his eyes, he asked me to call Mum.

I put him down slowly. I was afraid that when I came back, I would not find his eyes open. I called Mum's work. I could only say her name. A woman tried to calm me down. She kept saying that Mum had just left and would be there soon . . . and that everything would be fine . . . , it would be fine.

I quickly returned to Dad, but now he was almost ice cold.

'Diti, I want you to promise me something,' he said with great difficulty. He couldn't breathe anymore. 'Listen to Dad: if I have to die like everyone will one day, I want to go calmly. I will trust it to you.'

'Anything you want, anything you ask in the entire world, just don't leave me,' I hurried to say, 'Please Dad, don't leave us alone.'

'Look, honey. I don't want Rubin and Eri to seek . . . to revenge my blood. Let me say that. . . this is my greatest. . . desire. All right, Diti? You must not allow them to . . . for any reason.'
Then . . . he spoke no more. Then Mum came, along with my aunt and a crowd of people. The whole city had run to the hospital to give blood.

Like in the movies that I had seen many times with Dad, a doctor came in with his head down. He couldn't look at anyone when he said: 'I am sorry. We couldn't do anything.' He was talking about my dad. He was talking about my daddy."

No Hope in Man

I am disgusted with "The Mission of Blood-Feud Reconciliation". Now it is called "The Mission of National Reconciliation". They change offices, names, and posts, as if they are doing an extraordinary work. They call for meetings and covenants, they choose and get self-chosen— meanwhile in the land of my heart, multiply the families who have the 'Kanun' as their God.

Blood feud doesn't threaten his life anymore. Nevertheless, everything dawns and darkens the same. It is equally quiet, equally dead. But, why is it so now?

All the air I have breathed in my life I would call a waste, all the cycles of my growing, like most of the lucky human beings in the world, I would call nothing more than a wicked farce of this blind life. What is the meaning of this life? A universe of egos in an unstoppable war between spirit and body?

Is there hope, a trifle of hope for me, up there in the gigantic sky?

There is no emptier, more foreboding feeling than the one you live when, going against yourself, you set your desires upon something, and it disappoints you.

"If the soul is darkened
*   by a fear it cannot name,*
If a mind is baffled
*   when rules don't fit the game,*
Who will answer?
Who will answer?
Who will answer?"[3]

Hundreds of times, I mediate on these verses during the nights, when I put my head on my pillow, when I succumb to . . . Who will answer?

A Melody Still Playing

It took time, huh? It took time for me to convince myself that I had become ridiculous with this sickness of mine. You were my sickness.

The answer remained clear, sovereign, and proud. It bore the name of silence.

I couldn't study anymore. Not anymore!

I took time to mediate on the crumbled hearts of Diti, Lira, and Flavio. I lived with them. Like a foggy dream, the images and events of their days flickered across my face every day. No hand remained for me to grab. The foundation on which I had imagined my future was undermined; the value in which I had trusted every day was demolished little by little in front of my eyes.

Every verse I wrote held the inspiration of "Eri"; each book had the "Eri" dedication; every success or failure was motivated "by Eri"; I lived every dream and waking moment "with Eri". I was "the unreachable student", "the lightning journalist", "the beautiful daydreamer"; they called me "the sweet poetess"; me, "the volunteer of Blood-Feud Reconciliation", me–the person with an empty life.

While the gloom of dusk darkened to take the attention of destiny, life, or God—if, "by chance", there really was one—I started to see valium as my loyal friend, as the hands that I could grab. The desire to awaken on yet another morning slipped away as lightly as a tear on the surface of the desert.

I was beginning a show that would end with the throwing of the valiums down my throat. Yes, I was sure of what I was doing. I wanted them inside me, as deep inside me as possible.

While I was losing consciousness and everything was getting dark, just like every human being on his last breath, I felt afraid and broken in front of death . . . for what if life didn't end there? Yes, yes, because life doesn't die there!

Dana found me in my last weak moves. She gave the alarm in the dormitory and then immediately at the hospital.

They washed out my stomach to remove poison; they gave me back my life. I was drowsy, totally numb. With heavy eyes, I remember Mendi leaning his face on my hand and crying slowly, as if hiding. I was in that place where you start to understand the real weight of things and people, and you desire like crazy to help everything and everyone, but you cannot do anything for anyone.

I wanted to rest. When I would leave my bed, it would be to live like never before. Then and there I decided that I would even breathe air differently. I would take more time to enjoy it, slowly, harder.

My mother lived those days in a chair in front of me. From there she looked after me, from there she talked to me, distracted me, and made me feel better. She changed the compresses, fed me, dressed and caressed me, now gently taking plenty of time.

With my eyes closed tight, I heard her while she talked and talked, with her passion never getting tired.

"Melody, in the last days of my pregnancy, everyone wished and expected a boy would be born, because after all, he could carry on Dad's name... Well, we changed their plans, me and you. Immediately when you were born, your uncles, aunts, and our friends all bowed down in sadness. Dad was so angry that he wouldn't even look at you. Mum took you close to herself and hugged you softly. You were the most beautiful thing in this world. While I had you in my arms, you leaned your neck and put your small fingers between my hands. You were so fragile, so unprotected, so transparent, just like music playing on the harps of the heart and enticing the continuity of life. I didn't hesitate to call you Melody.

Free at Last

This is my last night at home. After that amazing ferry trip on the lake, this afternoon I will be sitting on the balcony of my apartment at the Campus. So, this is the last time I write to you, and it looks like this is also our last meeting point. Mendi will give Diti these notes which have taken the shape of a book. He promised that very soon they will be in your hands. I didn't ask how. Maybe he will mail them; maybe he will bring them himself.

Diti looks better. However, it remains visible how much he misses you and Rubin, like a need that life hasn't fulfilled yet.

Lira flew to Italy right after the ceremony of the third day in honor of your dad. And yet, I have the feeling that you know these things much better than I do.

Eri, it was exciting to start this journey with you, but now that I am reaching the end, though I'm tired, I don't feel like separating from it—maybe from the discomfort that I might have left something unwritten? Something important? Or because I know that abandoning these papers means fully separating from you? Maybe no less because of the feverish desire to know what will happen; how things will turn out?

If I have used the talent of combining words, though it hasn't been even the faintest motive behind these papers; if for whole nights I have remained alone "with you", on this worthless typewriter that gets on my nerves with its noise; if I have harmed family time, study time, and time with old friends, it has been a sacrifice; a sacrifice I would make again, any time it was needed, because . . . after every letter, there hides a desire; after each word, the same breath; after each phrase, my thoughts remain the same. And now you know very well what it is: the desire for you to avoid blood feud.

Unfortunately for me, time has the last verdict.

My hands are strolling now around the papers written since high school. My eyes meet pieces of sentences that immediately find their place in the drawers of memory. Here, I stop at the faded calligraphy of a poem:

Let me be a caress.
Let me be remembered by your soul's guitar
Let me be an angel,
As close to you, as to protect you, always.
If I was a candle,
I would endlessly meditate in your spirit,
I just want to be
Where you've never enjoyed anyone.

Freely I allow the landscape of the night when I created those verses for you to walk in my mind. You had asked me to dedicate something to you, and on that night, I felt and created these verses. The next day I put into your hands an entirely different thing.

A scared little voice inside me hadn't allowed me to trust you with this "wishful poem".
You seemed unreachable, beautiful but distant, sweetly eloquent. You were . . . a dream. Everything I had written until that night seemed only "a distant tone of a voice that I hadn't known".

But later on, you know . . . you know the whole story.

Eri, in the midst of hundreds of people walking around you, I would recognize your walk; in the midst of a thousand eyes, immediately I would find your eyes; in the midst of millions of people, I pray that this letter serves you as a MELODY— so that when you hear it, it instantly grabs you, there in that place and time, and makes you understand you have lost something. If along your road you lost me, don't despair!

If you are hurt by the voice that says you made me suffer, it doesn't matter anymore. They say some of the best lessons in life are learned from pain. And it is true.

Since the excellence of my mother's womb, when I was fearfully and wonderfully made, I have now found what I was looking for in you, the true Melody . . . the true meaning of life, because above all choices, deep in every feeling, at the end of every road, without Him, my soul would remain a desert that is occasionally drizzled with rain… an emptiness. Now I know, Eri- it is not me you miss there inside.

You miss love. You miss life itself. You miss what can fill you in silence and in fatigue, in rest and in loneliness. No rosebud of this world can match its beauty, and no thorn bush can… touch it.

If life offers you the chance to step once again in the land of your love, do not look for me, for I will not be there waiting. Not anymore. Not like I have been waiting. Nevertheless, I will be mentioning your name every day before Heaven, until the hard shell of your heart melts.

A Soul Transformed

"Somebody is looking for Melody!

"Melody Gjokaj, somebody is looking for you at the gate."

I put out my sleepy head and saw the girl who was almost yelling.

"Who's looking for me?"

"A certain Ermal, if I am not wrong. Yes, yes, he said his name was Ermal Korinaj," continued the girl whose face looked familiar to me. "What's wrong? Why do you make that face? Is he someone who has annoyed you? If so, I can go out and tell him you were not in the room."

Feeling good from her comprehension, I thanked her, "No, he is not one of those. If I had to complain, I would complain that he *hasn't* annoyed me," I said, without knowing why I was telling her that.

"Could this be one of Dana's jokes?" I wondered within myself. However, I didn't dare go out on the balcony and look. I was shaking in the deepest parts of my soul.

Instantly after these question marks, Dana came into the room, as lively as ten people. "Meliii, I saw Ermal. Where are you hiding? Melody, I have seen Ermal, I say! I recognized him from the photographs. I swear I almost fell down when I saw him. He was a sweetheart!"

In the meantime she came very close to me, and looking me in the eyes with admiration, she whispered:

"Finally you succeeded, Melody Gjokaj. You won. Fine then, as I am an expert on the works of the heart and I know how precious this moment is for anyone, and since I would go crazy from joy if I were in your place, I will leave you alone."

She went out of the room, and then poked her head back through the door:

"Hey, you can take whatever you want from my wardrobe, and make yourself beautiful like a star, all right?"

I was dizzy. My ears rang, turning and returning the sounds: "a certain Ermal, Ermal Korinaj." And unintentionally, unconsciously, I got lost in my expectations of long ago. I had desired this moment, hadn't I? Oh, how often I had imagined it!

I stood up instantly, instinctively glanced at myself in the mirror, and went out of the room. This was the moment.

Eri was sitting on a bench, his head bowed a little, with his eyes looking towards the door where dozens of girls were coming and going, where dozens of couples were kissing and caressing, talking and whispering to one another.

As soon as he saw me, he stood up and came close to me with a shy step, much shyer than in the past. He extended his hand, and then pulled me into his arms. A hug of lovers, who had longed to hug the body of their loved one, that's what it was. But it was also completely like a divine breeze that appears when two people whipped by life console, support, and understand each other.

We went to the coffee bar close to my dorm. As though he had been separated from all life, Eri followed my movements, like he lived for them alone. He gazed attentively on my every move and gesture; he rested his eyes on my face without saying a word, just like… just like high school.

"How are you, Melody?" He added with a sigh: "What a hypocrite I am, right? I hit you and then ask if it hurts?"

I didn't speak.

"I received the letters—or should I say, the book you've written. I have achieved so much: once I only asked for a poem, and today I have a book, a whole book for me. The meditations of high school times, your dreadful secret that I cannot even try to describe how hard it was on me, your unconsumed passion to keep me from hatred. . . I have read and re-read; I have devoured those papers, Mel. Every word, every letter, is poured onto those papers with the most beautiful art in existence: with love. I told you that you give life to everything. You forgot your days, years, friendships, even yourself, for me. Though I do not deserve your love, I want you to be sure that it will remain the dearest thing I have ever had. As for Elira . . . she has no blame, Melody. I have been the one who hasn't allowed her to speak about me, regardless of the fact that she wrote me in detail about you. I didn't know what I would do, I didn't know what I wanted, but I was sure that I wanted to be free from you. Free from the bewitching power you have on me. You know what? Lira sent me a picture of you. I cannot express what I felt when I held it in my hands and could gaze on you again, even though it was only paper. You were so beautiful . . . you *are* so beautiful. I enlarged that photo to a poster's dimensions, and I had you close to me every morning, like someone you want to be near to in every blink of the eyes. I slept and woke up with you. I rested and cried. We chatted, and I often talked to you like a person who speaks in delirium. I imagined the boys that dreamt of you and invented reasons to be close to you, while I, the one who had your heart, needed to leave it free for someone else. The girls I met looked like men to me. In the whole universe, there was only one girl for me, the one with the name of Melody Gjokaj. I remember knowing and writing that you were the best gift I had ever received . . . a gift that is impossible for me to keep. In me lives an entirely different Ermal, one I have never known, one who sometimes scares me."

His eyes became crystal clear from tears.

"You would never forgive me for what I'm eager to do. It is true- the only thing that would stop me is love. It is so, Melody; I have strained to erase you from my life, I have acted as though you didn't exist, and yet again I am convinced you will always be a seal on this . . . heart of mine. You're impossible to forget, Mel, but . . . the hatred I feel is greater and more powerful than love."

"Eri, you're saying that hatred is worthier to be lived than love is, that's what you are saying," I interrupted, and without embarrassment I gave free way to tears.

After all, I was facing what I had always feared. I started talking to him like I had talked to myself hundreds of times, strolling around my room in front of the mirror. Hundreds of times I had thought about and prepared for this as though it were the hardest and most important test of my life.

"Mel, I have come back to avenge my father's blood. Right now this is the only reason why I live."

"Eri, you want to kill, and in your way you will drag innocent people, people whose only sin is that they carry the Kikaj's name—children like Diti, and as guilty as Flavio. Don't you understand? Is this what you want to achieve? Is this the reason why you live? You will be part of that dirty game, which you once so diligently hated. Where is the Eri I have known, the one I have loved? What has happened, sweetheart, to make you erase everything you have been?"

"They killed my father, Mel. Haven't you heard?" he yelled, drawing people's attention.

"But nothing, no other murder would bring him back to life. You don't understand how vain, how ugly, how inhumane this is . . ."

"They have destroyed my family," he continued, disregarding my presence.

It was as though he had strapped his heart from his body, and now hatred and greediness had occupied its place.

"Elira has become crazy; Diti's childhood is ruined; I have a mother whose tears have not dried up for years. Don't you know?!"

"Look at me for a bit, please. Listen to me a little. Nothing you manage to do can fix the past, it can't be undone. So . . . how . . . what's the worth of destroying people's lives, not to mention your own?"

"Mel, I ask your forgiveness, forgiveness for the hurt, pain, and everything I've caused you, but please don't interfere."

"No, you are asking forgiveness with words only," I continued raising my voice, unable to control myself. "You are saying my suffering was in vain. You are turning your family's sacrifices to nothing, and you are inconsiderate of what happened to Elira. And all this just to become a criminal? Tell me then, what do you plan to do with your dad's last words? With what we call a "dying wish"—will you break it?"

"On the contrary. I am making justice," he replied, with a flash of assurance in his eyes.

"Before I leave, this time forever, I wanted to add one more detail to your book. And here it is," he said, leaving the famous diary on the table, "I will give it back to you. I will erase every memory, every object. I will destroy everything that connects me to you. Perhaps this way I will remember you less frequently.

"The day dad left for the Kikaj's neighborhood, he knew it was the last time he would see the sun. After all that time, he had managed to learn what had happened to Elira, why she abandoned school so suddenly, why so strangely she never visited him, why she got married so abruptly. A friend told him what being Luan Korinaj's niece had cost her. He had left home to kill someone, Mel, and naturally knew he would be slaughtered there. It is better that he . . . remained . . . in his beloved yard."

We stayed silent for some moments, wiping our tears without avoiding each other's looks. Then in a hasty change of face, as if he was not himself anymore, Eri added:

"What he didn't achieve, I will. They have butchered my family, and I will butcher theirs; they put me on the streets, now it's their turn. They will have it, they will feel grief within the pores of their skin. Lira was like a sister to me, so they will know what it feels like when their own sister gets dragged around, when she is violated and alienated forever. Their children will taste the terror that covers you when you see your dad torn apart by bullets in front of you, while he falls into your hands, as happened to my brother. Precisely for this reason I have come back. I came to avenge the one who gave me life, and I couldn't clean his flowing blood; for the dreams and nightmares that wake my brother up every night, for the scar Lira will always have on her lips and soul, for the un-dried tears of my mother. I have also come back to avenge my love, the one I was deprived of once and forever, because the most important part, the most beautiful part of my life is dying today, because . . . because, Mel, I love you the same as the day you promised you belonged to me.

"Well, then, Melody Gjokaj, I wish you all the best of this world. I am sure that He, your God, will take care of you."

He stood up, kissed me on the forehead, and whispered:
"Farewell, my sweetheart."

He called the waiter, paid for the untouched drinks on our table, and walked away in a hurry, without once looking back.

I was completely powerless in the face of this reality, and being numbed from helplessness, I couldn't feel the hurt in its fullness. When the numbness weakens, I know pain will be waiting for me.

Epilogue

This is my story, one of the most painful realities of the country I live in, the country I love. This is my drama. I don't know if there could be another limit to how deep blood feud has torn my heart. Deeper than where it hurt Flavio, than where it crippled Lira, deeper than where it transformed Eri? Could it possibly go any deeper?!

Flavio is taking care that his parents go to live where he is, abandoning Albania forever.

I haven't heard of Eri since that day. My city is gripped by something stronger than silence; I will call it a pause. I fear this is . . . only for a while.

The Melody of My Love is a book that begins as a romance and ends as a drama. It takes the reader aback with the truth of everyday pain and agony. Beyond its focal theme, the Albanian blood feud and the consequences that this terrible phenomenon causes in the spirit of Albanian society, the reader investigates the deepest battle of every human soul between life and death, hatred and love, good and evil. This battle is played openly on the realities of the character of "Melody". The drama closes with the expectation of a tragedy. The silence that follows after reading the final lines and closing the last page of the book causes the reader to expect a tragedy waiting to be played tomorrow or sometime in the future.

Her confession is conceived at times as a journal and other times as an epistle, so the reader looks deep beyond the events of the novel, into the soul of the characters who undergo a dramatic transformation because of death and hatred. The language used is mostly poetic. Due to the dramatic and painful events that are related, the reader understands the weight of blood feud in the life of a society. The author has joined together in these events life and death, love and hatred, turning the book into a "poem" of blood feud.

Endnotes

[1] Engjëll is an Albanian name for a male, meaning: Angel

 [2] "Kanun", or the "Canon of Lek Dukagjini", is a set of traditional Albanian laws originating from ancient Illyrian tribal laws and codified in the 15th century. Mostly used in northern and central Albania, it includes and honor code of conduct ("Besa") from which clan-based "blood feuds" arose. It was revived after the fall of the Communist regime in the early 1990's

[3] "Who Will Answer?" from the album *Who Will Answer*, Ed Ames, Shiela Davis (1967).

www.ingramcontent.com/pod-product-compliance
Lightning Source LLC
Chambersburg PA
CBHW070808120626
46557CB00002B/755